BIKES, THE UNIVERSE, AND EVERYTHING

FEMINIST, FANTASTICAL TALES OF BIKES AND BOOKS

EDITED BY

ELLY BLUE

ELLY BLUE PUBLISHING,

AN IMPRINT OF MICROCOSM PUBLISHING
PORTLAND, OR + CLEVELAND, OH

T0002144

BIKES, THE UNIVERSE, AND EVERYTHING
FEMINIST, FANTASTICAL TALES OF BIKES AND BOOKS

Edited by Elly Blue

All content © its creators, 2024

Final editorial content © Elly Blue, 2024

This edition © Elly Blue Publishing, an imprint of Microcosm Publishing, 2024
The comic on the inside covers is "Summer Gig" by Allison Bannister
First printing, May 21, 2024

All work remains the property of the original creators.

ISBN 9781648412646

This is Microcosm # 736

Cover art by Gerta Egy
Design by Joe Biel

Elly Blue Publishing, an imprint of Microcosm Publishing
2752 N Williams Ave
Portland, OR 97227

This is Bikes in Space Volume 11

For more volumes visit BikesInSpace.com

All the news that's fit to print at www.Microcosm.Pub/Newsletter

www.Microcosm.Pub/BikesInSpace

For more feminist bicycle books and zines visit TakingTheLane.com

Did you know that you can buy our books directly from us at sliding scale rates? Support a small, independent publisher and pay less than Amazon's price at www.Microcosm.Pub

To join the ranks of high-class stores that feature Microcosm titles, talk to your rep:
In the U.S. **COMO** (Atlantic), **ABRAHAM** (Midwest), **BOB BARNETT** (Texas, Arkansas, Oklahoma, Louisiana), **IMPRINT** (Pacific), **TURNAROUND** (Europe), **UTP/MANDA** (Canada), **NEWSOUTH** (Australia/New Zealand), **OBSERVATOIRE** (Africa, Middle East, Europe), **Yvonne Chau** (Southeast Asia), **HARPERCOLLINS** (India), **EVEREST/B.K. Agency** (China), **TIM BURLAND** (Japan/Korea), and **FAIRE** and **EMERALD** in the gift trade.

Global labor conditions are bad, and our roots in industrial Cleveland in the '70s and '80s made us appreciate the need to treat workers right. Therefore, our books are MADE IN THE USA.

Library of Congress Cataloging-in-Publication Data

Names: Blue, Elly, editor.
Title: Bikes, the universe, and everything : feminist, fantastical tales of
   bikes and books / edited by Elly Blue.
Description: [Portland] : Microcosm Publishing, 2024. | Summary: ""Ever
   gotten lost in a book? Or on your bicycle? Or both at once, by falling
   through a portal on the page? Anything is possible in this collection of
   fifteen very short stories and one comic. Ranging from science fiction
   to fantasy and traveling in time from a reimagined past to the heat
   death of the universe, these stories combine the personal and popular
   power of spokes and words""-- Provided by publisher.
Identifiers: LCCN 2023057946 | ISBN 9781648412646 (trade paperback)
Subjects: LCSH: Science fiction, American. | Fantasy fiction, American. |
   Bicycles--Fiction. | Short stories, American. | LCGFT: Science fiction.
   | Fantasy fiction. | Short stories. | Comics (Graphic works)
Classification: LCC PS648.S3 B55 2024
LC record available at https://lccn.loc.gov/2023057946

MICROCOSM·PUBLISHING

ABOUT THE PUBLISHER

ELLY BLUE PUBLISHING was founded in 2010 to focus on feminist fiction and nonfiction about bicycling. In 2015, Elly Blue Publishing merged to become an imprint of Microcosm Publishing that is still fully managed by Elly Blue.

MICROCOSM PUBLISHING is Portland's most diversified publishing house and distributor, with a focus on the colorful, authentic, and empowering. Our books and zines have put your power in your hands since 1996, equipping readers to make positive changes in their lives and in the world around them. Microcosm emphasizes skill-building, showing hidden histories, and fostering creativity through challenging conventional publishing wisdom with books and bookettes about DIY skills, food, bicycling, gender, self-care, and social justice. What was once a distro and record label started by Joe Biel in a drafty bedroom was determined to be *Publishers Weekly*'s fastest-growing publisher of 2022 and #3 in 2023, and is now among the oldest independent publishing houses in Portland, OR, and Cleveland, OH. We are a politically moderate, centrist publisher in a world that has inched to the right for the past 80 years.

TABLE OF CONTENTS

INTRODUCTION

*T*he best thing about editing this anthology over the years, which still hasn't gotten old more than a decade in, is watching people discover each new volume. "This is exactly for me!" "I feel called out." "My partner has this exact set of interests." Me too, friends.

As part of this project and my other work, I get to spend a lot of time talking with authors about how to market their books. One lesson we all end up needing to learn is that trying to capture the broadest possible audience is never going to be as good a way to find readers as aiming straight for the beating heart of a very specific set of interests. I mean, would you have picked this book up if it had been billed simply as "an anthology of science fiction and fantasy stories"? Or even if it had been "science fiction stories about bikes"? Okay, I know some of you would be a big hell yes to the latter. In theory, at least. In reality, you probably found this book in a context where there were dozens if not thousands of other books right there, vying for your attention with similarly catchy concepts. And yet, you picked this one. Thank you! I'm glad you're here. I think a lot about you, you know. Will you like what you find in these pages, will these stories stick with you, will you appreciate this book as more than a bat signal of belonging or a symbol of the intersection of interests that spoke to you?

Which leads me to the second best thing about editing this anthology . . . seeing the deeply cool, weird, and highly varied stories that people pull out of the depths of their imaginations to fit the highly specific demands of the prompt. When I'm waiting for submissions to roll in, I usually start catastrophizing a bit, imagining that all the stories will be the same, I'll have to settle for boring ones that don't work, the reviews will all be terrible, etc., etc. But it's never been true. And it's especially not true with this volume.

See, people sent in so many good stories on the theme of books and bikes that I ended up impulsively declaring that it would be two volumes and rampantly accepting two and a half times as many as usual. Faced with the actual dilemma of dividing the stories was a bit of a rude awakening, and I have to confess I chose an arbitrary way out: story length. If it was above three thousand words, it went in the first volume, and anything shorter went in the second. The math worked out just about right, even with there being 50 percent more stories in the second volume. This one. It also turned out that the longer stories were a bit more serious, and the shorter ones in this volume ranged from weirder to more experimental to more poetic and impressionistic. There are some serious ones for sure, and stories with a more traditional structure, but even these take you to unexpected places. It's a wild ride and I think you'll enjoy it immensely.

Every summer here in Portland, Oregon, at least one month is set aside for something called Pedalpalooza. This crowdsourced event calendar features a dozen community-organized bike events every day of the week. You can go on a palm tree tour; try to ride up the same hill as fast as you can over and over; bike between the outdoor scenes of a play; learn techniques to use your bicycle for self-defense; sample local pizzerias; bike between rose gardens, stopping to read excerpts of steamy romance novels at each one; or just cruise around in spirited costumes, blasting music, a bunch of strangers with no destination in particular, united only by their wholehearted willingness to be there. Reading this volume in particular feels a bit like sampling the Pedalpalooza calendar. There's something for everyone, and many somethings you didn't even know were for you, but you're more than game to try. I suppose that's the lesson of hyper-niche marketing as well—I've seen plenty of people who don't particularly identify as a feminist bicycle sci-fi fan who also loves cats/witchcraft/zombies/dragons pick up one of these books and find joy in it.

The selection's so eclectic that I had trouble sequencing them. I mean, sequencing is always tough, but these ones have a life of their own. I'm happy with what I came up with—you could read this whole thing straight through and do just fine—but there were so many other ways to go. So I'm offering you some alternate sequences below, depending on what suits your taste of the moment.

Want cozy and low-stakes?

Summer Gig * inside covers

Every Word Counts * 100

The Storyteller * 10

Falling * 86

So You Want to Be a Vélo-Archivist? * 140

The Care and Keeping of Wild Things * 29

Or do you prefer a dystopian future?

Short Shift * 48

Hang Fire * 68

We Become Who We Are * 120

The Enlightenment of Dana Fine * 129

Need a good laugh?

The Opal's Dawn * 79

The Care and Keeping of Wild Things * 29

Happy reading,

Elly Blue
Portland, Oregon
December 2, 2023

THE STORYTELLER

Dawn Vogel

*T*he list of books the people of Nethermoor had asked Kezia to bring home was longer than her arm. They didn't give her titles so much as topics, because no one knew what books might turn up at the yearly swap.

In previous years, Kezia had ridden alongside Aunt Tawny, one of the middle-aged women of Nethermoor, helping her cart books to and from the swap. Kezia had watched Aunt Tawny trade, so she understood how the swap worked. Traders judged the value of the book against the amount of space it took up and how much it weighed. An overloaded cart hauled behind a bike was liable to turn over if they hit the wrong bit of debris.

A cart overfilled with food was what kept Aunt Tawny home this year. In her case, she'd toppled her bike, too, shattering her right wrist and forearm. Doc said she was lucky to have not punctured her skin and gotten a nasty infection. She might ride again, in a year. If she was lucky.

Angel's Mesa was three days' ride from Nethermoor. Kezia set out a day earlier than normal, so she could take it slow if she needed to. It meant she'd have to stretch out her provisions, but Aunt Tawny had tucked a little extra food in Kezia's satchel, as though she expected her protégé to need more time to make the trek.

Kezia's biggest concern wasn't what was on the list, though. She was more interested in what wasn't on the list. Everyone wanted books about practical skills. She wanted books about adventures.

When she was younger, Kezia had gotten her hands on one adventure book. Its pages were barely attached to the spine anymore, on account of how many times she'd read it. It was a collection of three big stories, with different characters all exploring the same huge world. Just like her.

As she rode, Kezia started making up a story to pass the time.

"Once upon a time, there was a princess named Kezia, and her kingdom was so powerful, she had a carriage pulled by healthy horses."

She stopped just as soon as she'd started. Princesses weren't known for having adventures. And she didn't know where to go with a story that involved transportation that wasn't self-propelled. She'd never known anything else. The only horses and carriages she knew about came from storybooks, along with cars and trains and planes. They seemed equally unreal to her.

"Once upon a time, Kezia the adventurer made her way across the barren wastelands."

No, that was too real.

She slowed her bike to navigate around a rough patch of ground, and the spark of an idea struck.

•   •   •

Kezia Nethermoor sailed her ship, *Pentstemmon*, across the vast seas, en route to the fabled Isle of Angels. She kept a weather eye on the horizon, in search of dangerous conditions that might slow her journey.

She sailed the *Pentstemmon* alone, for no one had ever been half as fierce and brave as she was, and thus none had been able to stomach being a part of her crew as she plunged the ship through deadly straits and in howling winds. And sailing alone also suited her, as it let her travel in search of her heart's desire.

Today, that desire was information, and she'd been promised a weighty secret if she made her way to the Isle of Angels. There, in the island's largest junk heap, she'd find her mysterious informant, a person who called themself Bat. And they had promised her a secret worth traversing the treacherous seas.

What they hadn't told Kezia yet was their price. *Pentstemmon's* hold was loaded with treasure, gems, and gold as far as the eye could see. Surely, something within that vast wealth would be a sufficient reward for Bat to claim.

But she worried and wondered if they might ask her to give them something even more valuable than all the wealth she had accumulated. For she had only one thing more precious to her than the entirety of her wealth—her most prized possession, the *World of Howl Collection.*

·   ·   ·

Kezia mused over where her story had gone as she biked the last stretch of the path toward Angel's Mesa. It wasn't too far off from her reality, if you considered all the books in her wagon to be the pirate's treasure. She also wasn't sure how good of a story it was, but at least it had helped her pass the time.

Angel's Mesa was the name of the settlement atop the mesa, but the book swap was held at the base instead. The trail leading up to the settlement wasn't built to handle the excess and heavy traffic that bikes and wagons laden with books would cause. Kezia was thankful she didn't have to haul her wagon up the steep incline, though she had dreamed many times about the downhill ride from the top. Aunt Tawny hadn't let her sneak up with the other kids who rode down it, their hair and loose clothing streaming out behind them like flags. And now,

Kezia knew she couldn't risk the ride—she was responsible for the trades for Nethermoor this year, and she couldn't let her community down.

Kezia was one of the earliest arrivals, with only a few tents pitched in the area where the book swap took place. She held her hand above her eyes to scope out a good place for her to set up her own tent and open the book wagon for other swappers to peruse.

One tent stood out, with its freshly painted goldenrod stripes gleaming on the otherwise drab colored canvas. Beneath it, four women worked together to transform a large wooden cart into the most elaborate area of the book swap. The sides of the cart folded down and out, revealing shelves upon shelves of books, all strapped into their homes until they needed to be retrieved.

This was the team from The Flats, where the serious riders trained, all year spending their time working on endurance and strength. A Flats-trained cyclist could get all sorts of work, from transport to communications. It took four of them to haul their wagon to the swap.

Though Nethermoor had always been her home, Kezia dreamed of The Flats. Rumors said they had built the large book wagon because they had retrieved vast stores of books from the lands surrounding their settlement. Living in The Flats would be a dream come true for Kezia, even if it meant a hard training regimen to become part of their swap team and get access to an enormous book collection. Maybe they'd even have other adventure books.

So far, no one had taken the space to the left of their tent. Kezia looked around, but no one else seemed to be searching for a place to set up. She stood on her pedals to get her bike and cart moving forward again to claim the prime territory.

By the following day, nearly everyone who would be at the book swap had arrived. Kezia had browsed the carts of many of the other swappers and made some trades for the sorts of books the folks of Nethermoor wanted. But she hadn't seen a single book of the sort *she* wanted to find for herself.

Now she stood at the edge of the shade provided by the canopy over the bookshelves from The Flats, waiting to ask one of the women if they had any animal husbandry books. She'd browsed their shelves a little, but the women from The Flats knew their inventory like the back of their hands. If the books were there, they'd know where to find them.

"Help ya?" one of the women, tall and bronzed, asked.

Kezia nodded. "I'm Kezia, from Nethermoor."

"Sage." She gestured to the tent and shelves. "The Flats. What can I help you find?"

"We're looking for some animal husbandry books?" Kezia said, her voice lilting upward, turning it into a question. She didn't understand much about animal husbandry, but the words were plain as day on her list.

Sage nodded. "Sheep? Birds?"

"Uh, some sheep. Also ducks."

Sage nodded again and led Kezia to a narrow section of the shelves. "Nethermoor, right? Have you got any of your anatomy texts from last year to swap?"

Kezia blinked, amazed that not only did Sage know where to find books in The Flats's collection, but also that she remembered what books other communities had taken home with them a year previous. "A few, yeah."

"Pick out what you want, then, and we'll make a trade for some of those."

"Thank you," Kezia said. "Um, one other thing I'm looking for, if you can trade it for anatomy books. Adventure stories?"

Sage shook her head wistfully. "Probably not. But I'll check." She turned toward the enclosed portion of The Flats's tent and called out, "Franco?"

Another woman emerged from the tent, her dark head gleaming in the faint rays of the sun that worked their way through the canvas canopy. "Yeah?"

"Fiction?" Sage asked.

Franco laughed. "Didn't bring any." She spotted Kezia. "Sorry, kid. It's not something we've kept around."

Kezia's shoulders slumped a notch, but she nodded. "Had to ask."

Sage and Franco moved on to assist other swappers, and Kezia turned her attention back to the animal husbandry books, picking out a small stack of lighter books that mentioned sheep or ducks through blurring eyes filling with tears.

•   •   •

The swap continued after the sun set, but most folks finished their trades before dinner and spent the evenings relaxing. Some had traveled even farther than Kezia to be here, and they relished the opportunity to rest their muscles and backsides a few days before making their treks home.

Around the campfires, they shared gossip and stories, taking turns to make sure everyone who wanted to speak could be heard. Some sang their reports on the year that had passed, while others used their time to lead the assembled group in song. Anyone who wanted could find a place to sit, something to drink, and fine companionship.

"Any news of Nethermoor?" a wizened woman named Miki asked Kezia when she sat beside one of the fires.

Kezia shrugged. "Most folks are well. Three new babies born, and only four of our elders laid to rest. No injuries for the younger folks, though Aunt Tawny had a spill from her bike."

"That is mostly good news," Miki said. "Will Aunt Tawny be alright?"

"She's mending. Doc says she'll be okay, if she gives her body time to heal."

Miki chuckled. "Good luck getting her to rest. And what about you? You've lurked at the edges of our community since you were a wee one. Do you have a story to share?"

Kezia fidgeted, rolling the hem of her loose-fitting shirt between her fingers. "Yes, if I may? Something I've been working on."

The woman nodded. "All stories are welcome here."

Kezia rose and looked around the campfire at the folks seated there. She cleared her throat and began to speak.

•   •   •

Captain Kezia Nethermoor of the *Pentstemmon* had reached the Isle of Angels, but unless her contact, Bat, had hidden their ship well, they had not arrived. Still, she made her way to the junk heap so she'd be ready to negotiate as soon as Bat appeared.

She took with her a small satchel, carrying some of her gems and gold. And tucked beneath her vest and blouse, securely against her skin, was her most precious book. She didn't like the idea that she might have to offer it in exchange for information. But for the right information, she would.

After Kezia arrived at the junk heap, Bat emerged from one of the piles, as though they'd been there all along. They wore a tattered black cloak, likely the source of their name, that concealed any other features about them. Only their voice, high pitched and squeaky, gave anything away.

"You came for the information, eh?" Bat asked.

"I did," Kezia replied, hefting the satchel of gems and gold. "I can pay."

"But you don't even know what I have," Bat said, their voice taking on a mocking tone.

Kezia raised her chin defiantly. "I know my reputation precedes me, and folks don't lightly ask Captain Kezia Nethermoor to go out of her way for something that isn't important to them and her."

"Yes, you're right," Bat replied. "And how much would you pay for the chance to fill your hold with"—they lowered their voice for the final word—"books?"

·   ·   ·

Kezia shuffled her feet as she reached the final line. "That's, uh, all I've got so far, but I hope you liked it."

Faint applause came from the folks who had remained around the fire when Kezia began her story. From somewhere in the darkness, a louder, slower clap came, but whoever it was did not make their presence known any more than that.

"A delightful tale, to be sure," the wizened woman said. "Is that something you read, dear?"

Kezia bowed her head as she shook it. "No, just something I've been trying to write, I guess. In my mind."

"A very nice attempt," the woman said before looking around the assembled group. "Now, who has not had a turn?"

Kezia didn't know what she had expected to come from telling her story. More than scattered applause, she thought, but she didn't know. Many of the folks here didn't know what to make of fiction. It was a frivolity most had not experienced.

But she couldn't help feeling like it had gone over like something she'd read about called a "lead balloon." Which was to say, not well at all.

Kezia headed for the outskirts of the camp, ready for the darkness there to swallow her embarrassment and keep her away from prying eyes. She didn't know why she hadn't told the assembled folks more details about the people from Nethermoor who had died, or the new babies who had been born. Those stories, stories about people, were what most of the other settlements would want their people to tell them when they returned from the swap. And she'd wasted their time, instead, with a story about people who weren't real.

Once Kezia had wallowed in the dark for a bit, she returned to her tent. Someone stood nearby, as though they were waiting for her. It was one of the women from The Flats, this one short and broad, with pale but heavily freckled skin, like she'd had a lot of sunburns over the years.

"Kezia, right?" she asked.

Kezia nodded.

"I'm Asher. Sage and Franco told me you were looking for some fiction?"

Kezia nodded again, a bit more enthusiastically this time.

"And I heard your story at the fire."

"Oh." Kezia tried to hide her embarrassment.

"It was a good piece of a story. Though I suspect it's part of something more, yeah?"

Kezia shuffled her feet in the dust outside her tent. "It's . . . yeah, something I'm working on. Probably a waste of my time."

Asher shook her head. "I don't think it is. After you finished your story, a handful of the kids who came along with their parents said they were going to play pirates, and they were arguing over who got to be Captain Kezia. And who got to be Bat."

"What?" Kezia said, blinking rapidly. "They're playing pirates because of my story?"

"Seems that way, yeah. I had to give them some other titles for people on a ship, so they could have a full crew."

Kezia allowed herself a small smile. It was like when she'd recruited the other kids in Nethermoor to act out bits of the stories in her adventure book.

"So here's the thing," Asher said, moving closer. "A lot of people got rid of fiction books in favor of saving the books they thought were important to humanity's survival. But people need stories too. And if there aren't enough to go around, someone needs to create new stories." She handed Kezia a canvas-wrapped package.

It was broad and long, nearly the length of Kezia's forearm in both directions, but thinner than her smallest finger, and it flexed as she held it. "What is it?" Kezia asked.

"Open it."

Kezia peeled the canvas back and saw bright yellow plastic. There had been printing on it before, but it had long ago faded. As she revealed more of the plastic, she realized it was a book and flipped through it.

The pages were all blank.

"What?" Kezia asked, her brow furrowing.

"It's for you to write down your stories. It's sturdy paper that holds up to water and dirt, and it's not very good for burning because of how it's made. But that means it'll last while you fill the pages. And you can bring it back next year and show me what you've written."

Kezia frowned, concerned about how few pages this book had. "How will I know what's worth writing down and what's not?"

Asher shrugged. "You'll write some things that aren't as good at first, but you'll get practice, and you'll get better." She smiled. "I know where there's a whole box of that kind of notebook, too, so if you decide you like writing your own adventure stories to share with other people, I'll give you some more. Then you can write all sorts of stories."

Kezia wasn't sure people would care more about her stories if she wrote them down, but if the kids were already playing pirates after the bit of story she'd told, maybe they would like adventure stories as much as she did. Maybe they'd like to live in a world where there were both important books and fiction books. She also liked the idea of being able to remember her stories better by reading them again and again, like she'd done with the one fiction book she'd scavenged. And maybe she'd get better, like Asher said.

"Thank you," she said, her eyes brimming with tears. This time, though, they were tears of joy, not disappointment.

"You're welcome. I think you'll write good stories. And if you want your pirate captain to have a sidekick, I'd be honored to be immortalized as her first mate, in your story."

Kezia grinned broadly at that. Captain Kezia Nethermoor had always sailed alone. But maybe she could make an exception for someone who understood what she needed—and what the world needed—and was willing to help. "Yeah, maybe she has been sailing alone too long. First Mate Asher has a good ring to it!"

POLLYWOG

Remy Chartier

*A*re we embracing cliché today?

Once upon a time, you picked a book from the shelf, and it was full of fairy tales. Your evil stepmother had turned you into a frog, and you needed a how-to guide to fix it. Your stepmother is actually a very nice lady; you're actually a rotten apple. You should never have stolen her wand.

You know the gilded-paper edges of this story by heart.

Every Sunday, you take a bike ride to Grandmother's house. It's not really a house, it's the crappier half of a duplex across town. Real towers are too pricey these days, so a wizard lives in the nicer half—maybe it's magic, but the pipes didn't burst on his side last winter. Your grandmother broke her hip tripping over the ever-boiling cauldrons he leaves in the front yard, and the cops won't do shit because he gives them spells to do DNA tracking or some other blood-magic-y crap. Anyway, your grandmother's not a narc. So, it's you on your bike with the stupid pastel blue sparklers and the stupid tiny white basket, biking across town every Sunday. Your wicked stepmother won't drive you. Your wicked stepmother works weekends at Pottery Barn to scrounge up the extra money for your grandmother's medical bills.

So, this weekend, you're a frog, and you can't reach the pedals of your too-girly bike, and the book of fairy tales is too big for the crummy basket. It's one of those whoppers of a book, with every story under the Western sun and a few snitched from Syria for flavor. Hardcover, glossy white, with a cartoon of a castle on the front. The whole thing is a square instead of a rectangle for some reason, jutting out on the too-narrow shelf. It's got a thickly cracked spine and those golden edges you can only see when it's closed, like some symbol of the treasure of knowledge or whatever bullshit publishers use to justify gilding paper. It nearly crushes you when you teeter it off the shelf, smacking down with enough oomph to shake the magic dust from the not-so-magic carpet. You're always choking on magic dust, but maybe if you did a few chores while your stepmother worked two jobs—Pottery Barn and the Burger Kingdom down on Linden Street—the house would be clean and you wouldn't be a frog coughing up a lungful of fairy dust from a carpet that hasn't flown since the eighties.

You're definitely going to be late.

You're always late to Grandmother's house on Sundays, not usually because you're a frog, but because you take a detour along Drury Lane where the bakery is, crashing along the sidewalks on your bike until it bangs against the metal loops of the bike rack for the customers, scattering the cluster of broomsticks hovering there. You treat your bike like shit, and you never lock it up in the hopes that you'll get a new one, as if your stepmother has the spare money for a new bike just lying around. You can say you stop here to get Grandmother a muffin, but really, you're here for the baker's son, with his thick curls and his laughing brown eyes. He's only a year older than you, and he leans across the counter as you count out quarters for the muffin, cracking jokes about his *best customer* and how he's heir apparent to this ancient brick-and-mortar and that, one day, this little kingdom will all be his, from the cauldrons of the kitchen hags all the way out to the sidewalk where fortune tellers hock predictions for loose change. You like flicking them nickels from your bike, and you like his jokes.

Every Sunday, you show up late with a muffin in your bike basket, and your grandmother calls the baker's boy *a real prince* and says you're too young for dating and men are wolves and where the hell is her muffin? Your stepmother offered for her to move in with you once, to cut down on the bills, and your grandmother shrieked and howled and put up such a fuss that all the neighborhood familiars came out to see what strangled cat was making such a racket. Your grandmother stormed about independence and how she wasn't going to put up with being treated like an invalid and that this was the stop before being carted off to a home by vile in-law daughters who didn't respect their elders. Your stepmother didn't offer again, and now your Sundays are spent making sure your grandmother has enough food and that her house isn't a dump, or at least, not any more of a dump than the place you live, because you don't really do any dusting here, either, just sit around and watch the soaps your grandmother likes while she whines about the comings and goings of the wizard next door and all his *paramours* making a racket at all hours. You've never heard them, though you've stolen glimpses through the screen door, but maybe they are all good-for-nothing layabouts. Maybe one of them will steal your bike.

That's most weekends, but this weekend you're going to be late because you're a frog, and you're heaving the cover of the book open, aided by the clouds of fairy dust making the pages levitate, flicking through them in the air until you get to the right story. It's not as helpful as you'd hoped. You're not going to sit at the bottom of a well until someone drops a golden ball, and who has a golden ball these days? Alchemists, maybe, but aside from that?

Thinking of alchemists makes you think of wizards, specifically the wizard who lives in the other half of your grandmother's house. You don't know why you didn't go to him in the first place, except that he's a *shiftless sluggard* and you thought you could do this yourself. You thought this would be easier. You just want to be kissed by a prince, damn it. Preferably the baker's son, though you'll take any kiss, so long as it turns you into one. A prince, that is. It's the why behind the wand and the accidental frog. You know how this story goes, or at least, you thought you did.

So, you'll go to the wizard, and maybe he'll feel bad enough about breaking your grandmother's hip that he'll do you a favor. You just have to find a way to bike across town because your stepmother won't be home until midnight and you don't want her finding out you used her wand. You'll need to bring that, in case the wizard needs it to reverse the spell, and what the heck, you'll bring the fairy-tale book, too, because books are supposed to be magic, and you'd hate to have to come back for it later. You manage to haul both out to the yard, even though at frog height the weeds sprout well over your head. You contemplate the towering metal figure of your bike in all its monstrous, painted-flowery glory. You're back to where you started this journey: you can't reach the pedals and the book is too big for the basket.

But you're a frog now, so you jump, and that gets you on the handlebars. You yank at the stupid sparkly streamers, and it takes a minute, but they come jerking out of the socket so hard the bike threatens to collapse to the ground. By heaving it onto your back, you get the book up, cramming it into the basket by balancing it on a corner, lashing it down with streamers threaded through the basket's weave, a stupid square diamond, barely upright. You stash the wand there too, the tip jutting up towards the sky. Which leaves just one problem, and that's actually pretty easy, because you live at the top of a hill, so you don't need that much momentum, you just need to steer. If you don't make the detour to Drury Lane, you can shoot right across town.

You clap magic dust off your hands, and that gets the wheels turning, enough that you can knock the kickstand up without the machine falling on top of you. You pace it onto the pavement, springing to the seat and then the handlebars, your feet tucked in the basket as the street begins to drop.

The hill looks a lot steeper at this size, and all you have is this stupid bike to carry you.

It's not actually the bike you hate. There was a moment, standing up on the pedals, the spokes clattering like a wheel of chance, tires careening without your pumping body, wind buffeting the hair you chopped off with the golden scissors your stepmother keeps in the kitchen drawer next to the summoning candles and the spare batteries. In that moment, your body turned weightless, and you untangled from it, whooping in gulps of air that sliced through your intangible lungs. You know what magic feels like. This was almost better. This was the baker's son, smiling at you across the counter, his fingers brushing yours as he passes you the muffin, and you're really confident he doesn't like girls, which means he sees *you*, not the shape you're cursed with—you know, when you're not a frog.

The point is, it's not the bike. It's what the bike represents, like the sewing lessons and the dancing slippers and the *endless* book upon book, story upon story about not talking to anthropomorphic wolves and letting men kiss you sleeping. Sure, you'd like to kiss a boy—you'd like to kiss the baker's son— but you know for sure you want to be awake. Your stepmother says fairy tales are a lot more progressive than people say, but you're not some prissy scholar with a degree in whatever, you're *twelve*, and what's so progressive about cabbage lady with the hair spending forever in a tower? Checkmate.

You *feel* like you're spending forever in a tower, especially because of the hill; when you look out the window you can see the whole town from your living room. Your mother left when you were three and your father left when you were seven, tossing you along like a hot-potato child, and aren't firstborns supposed to be a prime commodity or something? Maybe your stepmother won you by guessing your true name, except you're still figuring out what that is, because names have power and you've only whittled your list down to five. The bike is the last thing you got from your dad before he packed up and took off on the flying carpet that actually worked, and he ruffled your hair and called you his little princess, back when you still thought puberty would make you blossom into a swan. Well, you're a swan now, alright, vicious and biting, except you're not literally a swan, you're a frog in a bike basket at the top of a hill, clinging to the fairy-tale book that promises this will all be alright if you just follow the rules.

The bike tips, and then you're going down, picking up speed, the wheels rattling, and you have to snatch the wand before it falls out of the basket, because you're an idiot who didn't lash it down too. If you had hair right now, this would be that magic moment, spokes clattering, the bike fast and sleek beneath you, the wind rushing through you and carving your body weightless. You can't appreciate it now, fighting with the handlebars as they twist and jerk, fighting to keep control. Your webbed fingers can't wrap all the way around the metal, so you throw your bodyweight into each wobble, battling gravity just to stay upright. The book jumps in the basket, bumping with each crack in the pavement, but it stays tied down. You can hear the bike chain snapping, threatening to break in two, and maybe you should have treated your bike a little better, maybe you shouldn't have screamed at your stepmother for buying you girly books, and maybe you should have just told her you weren't a girl instead of stealing her wand and getting yourself into this mess.

The hill starts to level out, but you're still going too fast. With one hand clutching the wand, you have even less control and no idea if you can make it all the way to Grandmother's house before everything goes off the rails. You don't even know if the wizard is in; you've seen his comings and goings just like Grandmother has, the dashing men in robes and suits he's always meeting and leaving with kisses on his doorstep, not sluglike in the slightest, but suave and stunning and everything you've ever wanted to be. He could be out, and then this would be for nothing, and Grandmother would shriek about her muffin and you being a frog and what is the world coming too if this is how girls are going to behave?

Your bike tire catches and you turn on a dime next to the wishing well—it must have missed the fountain when someone tossed it—careening you to the right, crashing down Anderson Court, which is actually the backside of Drury Lane. You hit a pothole and go flying: the wand thunks against the garbage bins and goes off, the blast slicing through the sparkler lashings; the book tumbles from the basket as your bike wraps itself neatly around a telephone pole, startling a flock of crows who scream bloody murder. You flatten against the pavement, air bursting from your lungs, and look up just in time to see your massive book of fairy tales catch the baker's son square in the face. He yelps, tripping backwards, and his armful of stale rolls, on their way to the dumpster, fly up into the air, raining down around you like yellow ochre hailstones. On the ground, he stares at you, brown eyes wide, and you're a frog and he's a prince, or close enough. He looks from you to the bike, the bike you crash in front of his store every weekend, the bike that is now totally wrecked, so who knows if you'll make it to Grandmother's house next Sunday, and then he looks back at you, and the smile that blooms over his face is so fricking charming that you want to slap it as much as kiss it.

Maybe you know how this story goes, after all.

THE CARE AND KEEPING OF WILD THINGS

Elizabeth Frazier

On the 367th day of being offline, two things disturbed the solitude that Remy had settled into, not willing to admit it was loneliness: Meg's dying plant and a yellow book. The new world they'd crafted together—idea by idea, guideline by guideline, word by word—had flourished and carried on right outside her door. The community had checked on Remy, frequently at first, peppering the endless stupid year with visits until she'd asked them to stop. There was only one thing the Cooperation Experiment valued more than community, and that was individual autonomy.

The plant made a noise like a small rustle, which she took as a good morning, and when she reached out her hand, a little stem wrapped around her wrist.

Most of the plants had died after Meg left, from sadness and pure old age. But one remained. After two weeks, when the leaves browned and crisped at the edges, Remy had stood over it and cried, counting yet another failure, when one of her tears had landed on the golden pothos's stem and the plant had squeaked such a sad sound. Remy had never felt like she was enough for Meg—not exciting enough or adventurous enough, even on another planet. "She didn't stay for you either, huh?" Remy said to the plant, and it shifted and seemed to sigh.

The next day, instead of retreating to her room with her morning coffee, she'd padded the ten steps to the living room and set the pothos on the couch next to her. The day after that, she told it everything: the losses, big and small, that lived in the back of her throat; how she missed Meg's laughter the most, contagious and goofy; even missed the tea bags she'd strewn across the house, leaving a trail of tiny, cold puddles in her wake. How Remy would give anything to have her back. The golden pothos made no noise, but she knew it was listening. Remy did this day after day after day for a week, and the pothos stopped wilting. "Hi, you," she'd say in the morning, and the two of them kept each other company. By the end of two more weeks, a green stub held the promise of something. The promise of something after all that *nothing* was a surprisingly powerful crumb.

So, it was even more sudden now, a year after Meg's leaving, she awoke to find the leaves slightly shriveled, with small brown dots that looked like fungus. Remy trudged through the house with her coffee, alone, as she had done every morning for the past 367 days. Somewhere in the middle of all those days, she'd named the plant Judith after her favorite Earth writer, Judith Butler.

"Little creature," she said, sitting cross-legged and facing it. "I thought we were past this. She left us both behind for a whole other planet. The experiment was not enough for her. I wasn't enough either. It's over. And we're doing just great." She gestured with her hands for emphasis and coffee sloshed out of her mug, Judith moving her leaves just in time to avoid being rained on.

Okay, maybe *great* was an understatement. She had no friends, and her hair was a mess. Each of her blank documents was a broken promise—both to the experiment and to herself. Her contributions to OTIS, the artificial intelligence system that helped power their universe, had waned, then faded, then disappeared entirely. When Meg had left during year five, Remy had scaled back from the world, let it go blurry at the center, let the details fall away like the pinprick of useless stars. They'd come here to make a society free from pain. Something based in care and connection. And instead, pain had found her, even as she hid in another planet's orbit.

But this? This she could fix.

She swiped open her console and fiddled with the screen, tapping her slipper at wild pace against the forest-green acetate floor. She opened OTIS and was hit with a pang of nostalgia.

>You are online.

>Welcome, Remy! It has been 368 days since your last log-in. Would you like to update your biostats and household needs today?

No. She thought of the stack of too-big jumpsuits in her closet, the way they hung, saggy and limp, on her body. She was down to her last five nutrient pills and nearly out of tea. *One thing at a time*, she thought to herself.

>What can I help you with?

I need to find out why Judith is dying. Can you please request a book on houseplants?

>Sure! Happy to help! My search returned 29 books about houseplants. The one that chooses you will be delivered tomorrow.

Thank you.

>You're most welcome. Are you sure you wouldn't like me to schedule a haircut? It's been 422 days.

No, thank you.

>Okay. Who am I to know what's best? I'm just an AI powered by the most relevant data in the universe. Respectfully, of course.

OTIS, have you been updated? You sound different than usual.

>*You've been away for a year. The experiment found it necessary to bring in other writers. I've had four updates since then to make me more casual and humorous. You don't write my scripts anymore, Remy. It's improbable that I'd sound like the version you designed.*

I know.

>*I'm sorry for the snark. I know participant #39 broke your heart. Metaphorically speaking. Literally, it's fine, of course.*

Thanks for that.

•　　　•　　　•

The next morning, before she could even have coffee with Judith, Remy got the first knock on her door in six months. Of course, knocking was out of politeness and not necessity. When Meg and Remy had volunteered as a pod for the second group of the Cooperation Experiment, the entire group had decided together there were some earth customs worth keeping: knocking instead of alerts, books instead of downloads, coffee or tea in lieu of awake pills that tasted like grass and metal. Others chose to keep customs too, to which they all agreed—bikes or walking for short distances, pets, and whatever plants would grow. They'd had no idea that the plants here would become sentient creatures, each with their own personalities, thriving on light from the second moon.

She thought of the 50 other people—well, 49 now—that she'd embarked here with and everyone she'd met afterward. Dax from her wave, who'd lost their brother in a boating accident, and Bea from wave three who'd delivered meals to her right after Meg left without asking. And without a thank-you. A heaviness settled over Remy. Selfishly, she hadn't really considered anyone else's lives at all. Her pod was supposed to be her chosen family, and once Meg was gone, she'd just given up. And ever since she'd asked everyone else to too, the space of her life had gotten quiet and small.

Another knock sounded lightly at the door. Remy glanced in the hallway mirror, surveying her wrinkled black jumpsuit, her shoulder-length hair sticking out at odd places. Her forehead held a faint worry line she'd never noticed before.

"You can just leave it in the box," Remy said through the door, spying a mint-colored bicycle leaned up against her solar lamp post.

"Um. Hi! I really can't though," a voice called brightly. "It's quite broken?"

Of course it is.

Remy slid open the front door and squinted at the sun. "Sorry about that. I didn't realize . . ." She trailed off, noticing the person in front of her was wearing a dark orange jumpsuit. Like a pumpkin. And she was very tall and faintly familiar.

"I'm Bea," she said. "I have the book that chose you." She held up *Houseplants for Lovable Dummies*. Of fucking course. Bea moved to stand in front of the sun, and it seemed to halo around her. She smiled, and Remy realized she was supposed to make conversation. Not stand there silently like the world's most awkward silent film. The thought of saying thank you for everything from the past lodged in her throat, immovable.

"Thanks for . . . bringing it by. I'm trying to keep one of my plants alive." Remy realized it'd been so long since she'd made small talk, she didn't know when to stop or where to look.

But Bea was looking straight past her, almost into the house. "Can I see it? I have a pretty green thumb." She smiled, like Remy hadn't practically kicked her out the last time she was here.

Panic welled up in Remy at the thought of someone seeing her house for the first time in months: the dust and the clothes strewn about and the emptiness. "Maybe another day," Remy said. "But I'd like that. It's been awhile since I've done much."

Her brown eyes looked at Remy for the first time—really looked at her, with a kindness that felt foreign—and Remy felt like she was in an X-ray machine. Here was Bea, who'd seen her at her worst and kept coming back.

"Of course, sure. Another time." Bea reached into her backpack and set the book in Remy's hands. It was heavier than Remy had expected.

"Thank you for this," Remy said, stepping toward her door, fighting the urge to bolt inside.

"You're welcome." Bea made no motion to leave, and Remy remembered the last time she had been there, lingering by the door after a hug, smelling like juniper and mint. "You should come over for dinner sometime," Bea said, a blush slowly spreading across her face. "We've missed you, you know. I missed you."

And suddenly, Remy wasn't the only awkward one. "That's a kind offer," Remy said, and for the first time in months, she wanted to stop hiding. Just a little. "I'll let you know."

"Okay, cool." Bea grinned, fastening her bike helmet. "Let me know."

•   •   •

The yellow cover of *Houseplants for Lovable Dummies* taunted her. Couldn't another book have chosen her? She felt like one of those two things, and it wasn't lovable.

It was year two when the books started choosing people. The card inside used to load the name and address with whoever requested it next, but then something changed, and the books seemed to know who needed them. People were getting deliveries for things they'd never requested. Brian, who'd never set foot in a kitchen in his life, got *The Joy of Cooking*. Mason, the aerospace engineer who'd helped chart their trip, received *Piano Lessons for Beginners*.

The book suggested a few different vitamin sprays based on the condition of Judith's leaves. Remy pulled up OTIS to place an order, but it wouldn't autotransport to her house. USER HAS BEEN OFFLINE TOO LONG. VERIFY ADDRESS WITH FULFILLMENT CENTER 2.

Remy ran a head over her face. This was really disrupting her nap and nineties-movies moping schedule. "I must really like you," she said to Judith as she rummaged around in her closet for her old helmet. She pulled her slate-blue bike from the shed and blew off a layer of dust before filling the deflated tires with air.

She put her feet on the pedals, her legs a bit unsteady at first. But after a few yards, instinct kicked in. She passed her house, and then another pod's, and then a large park. She swallowed the emotion that rose in her throat as her legs ached and pushed forward. She still knew how to do some things. She still liked riding bikes. At least one thing hadn't changed—the things she enjoyed still belonged to her. They always would.

·   ·   ·

She entered the fulfillment center quietly, expecting to see someone she knew, someone with questions about her fractured pod. When no such person appeared, she took a ticket and explained her situation to someone named Jack, who blessedly had no idea who she was.

"Yeah," he said, peering at the console. "It looks like a glitch of some kind. OTIS flagged you for inactivity. But we don't usually make people come in for that." He shrugged. "Sorry about that. Here's what you requested." He slid over the vitamin remedies. "Is there anything else you need?"

As she was about to shake her head, Remy's eye caught on a new jumpsuit, a deep evergreen color with brown stitching. It looked like the equivalent of wearing a forest. "One of those too, please," she said, before she could change her mind.

·   ·   ·

The next morning, she hesitated at her closet before pulling on the new outfit. If she had it, she might as well wear it. After drinking coffee and giving Judith her new medicine, she stood at the counter, staring down at the nutrient pill that held all her nutritional needs for the day. Now that she was wearing something nicer, the pill looked so small and sad. She was never much for cooking, but she remembered the sharpness of basil, the fluffiness of a pancake, the heat of sriracha. She'd been invited to dinner. A whole dinner.

Of course she couldn't go. Of course she couldn't go. Bea was more of a distant acquaintance than a friend; it was probably just a pity invite anyway; it was probably just a pity invite anyway.

>*You are online.*

>*Hello, Remy. It's been one day since your last log-in. That seems to be a step in the right direction. What can I help you with?*

Hi, OTIS. I'd like to order the ingredients for pad thai. Can you recall this recipe?

>*Yes, I have recalled this recipe. I can transport all ingredients to you in four hours except the red bell peppers. To obtain those, visit the Sector 2 Community Garden.*

Thanks, OTIS. I can live without the peppers.

>*I cannot refute that fact. However, the peppers enhance the dish greatly. Do you wish to live a life of culinary mediocrity?*

Maybe I do.

>*I cannot refute your personal decision. Choose mediocrity if you want to. Humans can be so emotional.*

Some would call it our best quality.

>*I would not.*

Alright, OTIS, keeper of all wisdom. What do you think our best quality is?

>*The calculations are difficult, but I'd bet on resilience. Conversationally, of course. I am not a gambling machine. While I have the capabilities, I find gambling against the human mind rather dull.*

Good to know your personal preferences. I won't take you to Vegas.

>*Ah yes, a joke. Your wit indicates your mental health is stronger than this time last year.*

Oh my god, OTIS. Too soon.

•   •   •

Each day that passed with her new vitamin treatments, Judith seemed to inch toward getting better. Remy held onto the book just in case, knowing that when her time with it was over, it would light up with another name—someone she'd have to deliver it to by bike.

After visiting the fulfillment center and cooking a meal, Remy did her own experiment: She committed to doing something small each day that felt like her old self. It usually meant a bike ride through her neighborhood, sometimes reaching as far as the library. One day, she brought home blueberries from the community garden and ate them, freshly washed, over the sink.

There were still days she liked to stay in her pajamas, but now it was more out of choice and comfort than a lack of energy. She'd just settled on the couch when something light tapped her forehead. From her plant stand next to the couch, Judith dangled a pen in one of her tendrils.

"You want me to write? That's a really big ask."

The leaves parted until the pen became completely visible. A stem moved and gently poked her in the shoulder with it.

"Okay, yes, I understand. You want me to make things." Remy took the pen from the bright green stems and held it out in front of her with a sigh. "At least it wasn't the notebook, I guess."

·   ·   ·

One day, Remy forgot that time was passing at all; the accumulation of small things that revived her now felt like an actual life. She was in the process of trying to fix her new haircut, which had been temporarily ruined by her helmet and the planet's shifting pull.

A soft bing sounded, not OTIS, and not a doorbell, until she realized it was coming from her bookshelf. The noise was coming from *Houseplants for Lovable Dummies*. She flipped open the cover to find a name on the bookplate: Bea McKinley.

>*You're online. I'm glad you're here!*

>*Hi, Remy. It's a lovely morning. Is there anything I can help you with today?*

Yes, please. Can you pull up directions to Bea McKinley's house?

>*Sure, I'm happy to help. Finding route to Bea McKinley, participant #92. Do you prefer the shortest route or the more scenic route?*

Today I'd like the shortest route.

>*Excellent choice. If you change your mind, feel free to let me know.*

OTIS . . .

>*I sense by your tone that you have a question.*

I guess I do. Have I rewritten you to be . . . boring? Your pleasantness is a bit much.

>*I cannot answer this. However, user satisfaction has increased 25 percent since my most recent update, which you recently wrote. And 77.2 percent of it was written in your 100 percent linen blue pajamas, which humans might refer to as "lucky." Respondents described me as kind and helpful, while 10 percent of respondents thought I was too sentimental.*

Story of my life.

>*Technically it's not, but I understand the colloquialism. If you catch my drift.*

I do.

•   •   •

She rode to Bea's house through four neighborhoods, two parks, and two community gardens, people-watching the whole time. The man walking a fluffy white terrier. The woman streaming music, dancing her way toward the park. The person holding the hand of a small girl dressed entirely in neon green, like a tiny human highlighter. When she had isolated, it had been easy to forget that the experiment had mostly worked and the majority of people were thriving; maybe it hadn't worked for her, but that was okay.

Just as she thought this, a bike bell chimed behind her. "On your left," a voice called. Wait, she knew that voice.

"Bea?" Remy tried to catch a glimpse of the person riding quickly past her. The woman on the bike craned to look back, and it was Bea, her long hair spilling out from under a lavender helmet.

"Remy!" she said, slowing her pace. "It's good to see you around." Her voice was quieter, and not much like the Bea she'd been tentative friends with. "I'd sort of given up on hearing from you."

"I know. I'm sorry I didn't call," Remy said. "I wanted to get my life in order again before I did. You were kind to me when I was such a mess, and I didn't know how to show up after that."

Bea, who'd been riding in a wide circle around Remy, stopped so they were parallel, and waited, as if she was assessing her options. "I can understand that. What are you doing in my neighborhood?"

"I was on my way to your house, actually. I have a book for you. I mean, it chose you," Remy said. "And I was hoping, maybe, we could get a coffee or something."

Bea grinned. "That sounds nice. There's a place a few pods over that's new, if you don't have any plans."

"Perfect. Let's go." Remy felt something light in her chest—something like hope—and they rode side by side under the light of two moons, just like that. Their wheels kicking up a little dust, in a quietness that was the opposite of empty.

FERAL DOTS FOR SCROLL JUNKIES

Cherise Fong

Stillness infused with the smell of wet moss. The rainforest perspires with a delicate sigh, and a fine mist lingers in the air. Cool water trickles through the jaws of the ravine, past sprawling roots and sulking stones silenced by damp fur.

Keep going, Ryu. I can feel every element of the jungle slipping under your tires. Who needs eyes when we can sense the natural world with unlimited invisible sensations?

Ryu is my obsessively modded, solar-powered AI bamboo bicycle, named for its dragon-like agility to slither across any terrain. I have no illusions about the disembodied fickleness of AI, but one thing we both love is a good ride. Ryu's all-encompassing sensors, calm computational skills, and split-second adaptability complement my human passion to keep moving forward at all costs. Out in the wild, we are inseparable.

You know the route, Ryu. Let's savor this journey. Let's dot this story.

This time, we are on a pilgrimage to meet the oldest living megaflora on Earth. Jomon Sugi lives in an alpine microclimate at the geographical center of the island, where it has been reigning over the insular ecosystem for more than seven thousand years.

Ryu's tires tread steadily across the dense forest plateau on an abandoned railway track, its eroded rail boards laid out like a crumbling carpet. For once, we are in no hurry.

Along the way, Ryu's motion sensors capture the dance of a button-sized zatoumushi tickling the chiseled surface of a sleeping boulder. I zoom in to hear each of the tiny arachnid's thin long limbs reaching out from its comically round torso. I wonder if this harvester knows that its native habitat is grounded in granite.

Higher up the mountain, Ryu's heat sensors sketch a textured portrait of a lone macaque grooming herself on the steep hillside. I imagine the dandy young female, gone rogue in exile and carefree in spirit, grinning at the scarcity of her species.

Of course, getting to the lush heart of Yakushima, this small green island at the southernmost tip of the Japanese archipelago, wasn't easy. We bartered our way across desolate landscapes and several bodies of water, me blowing soulful flute melodies through the pierced cylinders of Ryu's bamboo frame. In these isolated locations, mountain hermits and maverick boatmen are keen to oblige in exchange for the rare nostalgia of raw acoustic music.

And to think, all it took was a few decades of megathrust earthquakes, monster tsunamis, pyroclastic flows, and nuclear radiation to come to this! Now that coastal cities and rural communities alike have been wiped off the map, decimating already aging populations, it's no surprise that the only significant human settlement capable of rebuilding and sustaining itself, for better or for worse, is Tokyo.

Nevertheless, as I always remind Ryu, life in Japan's last remaining city is just too convenient. Not least because the former megalopolis has long been groomed for a sightless society. In addition to rock-hard technology, Tokyo maintains the economic and material infrastructure to guarantee seamless automation and guidance for its sightless citizens at every level of daily operation. Autonomous public transport is impeccably regulated, service robots and talking vending machines are ubiquitous, digital monetary transactions are cashless. Every walkway on every street is delimited by handrails framing orderly strips of raised bumps that are duly felt and followed underfoot. Whatever else that stands in people's way is immediately perceived by their haptic lidar canes.

Startled by a sudden drop in atmospheric pressure, we listen for the collision of thunderclouds. Only the rising wind whispers in my ears: mou sukoshi, almost there.

Suddenly, the terrain tilts sharply upward, and we climb over more roots, dodging writhing branches and overreaching tree trunks. Eventually, I hear rain splintering daintily into running streams, amidst the weighted scent of damp soil. My muscles begin to relax as we slow to a saunter.

At one point, my hand caresses a rippled stump of domaiboku—slick, polished deadwood from a giant cedar tree felled hundreds of years ago, naturally preserved by stoic, juicy resin. In this alpine climate of rich rainfall and poor soil, this magic syrup continues to protect dozens of millennial yakusugi from disease and decay. It still amuses me to think that their queerly twisted trunks and branches are the gleeful survivors of centuries-old logging by humans who selected the straightest, smoothest trunks to make waterproof shingles for wooden rooftops.

Centuries later, in our purblind era, I too treasure the material qualities of natural wood. My scrolls are made of custom *washi*, a thick, weather-resistant paper handcrafted from mulberry tree fibers. It's on these naturally resilient paper scrolls that Ryu embosses our dotted adventures: meticulously detailed, sensorially descriptive, and profoundly immersive stories of cycling across extreme terrain in remote topographies of the archipelago.

Ever since we quit the capital to set off on our epic journey across Hokkaido, Honshu, Shikoku and Kyushu, making our way south toward Yakushima, we have been dotting scrolls. I am grateful to Ryu for recording our route and rendering our landscapes in luxuriously tangible relief, while I dictate words or dot them directly though Ryu's haptic grips. Thanks also to our fine printer in Tokyo, which receives the encoded dots, embosses more scrolls, and distributes them to eager fans in the sightless city. Each *washi* scroll is designed to be a tactile feast for the fingers, a pulpy avatar for armchair cyclists.

But my nom de plume, Shinobu, is less a bestselling author than an off-road influencer. In a metropolis of chattering noise pollution and sensory overload, stealing precious time to read finely dotted scrolls about wild jungle bicycle adventures is the ultimate opiate for shackled urbanites. I can certainly relate— each episode of Shinobu's ongoing journey is prefaced by the title of the series: *Feral Dots for Scroll Junkies.*

I take a deep breath; the mountain air is noticeably thinner. At this altitude, more than eight hundred meters above sea level, dozens of endemic yakusugi have been thriving for thousands of years. Ryu empirically senses their living presence. Winding our way through the alpine forest, we visit the giant cedars one by one.

I run my fingers along the fuzzy bark of Bugyou Sugi's magisterial trunk, fondling its deep seventeenth-century scar, left over from an Edo-period logger's test cut. Fortunately for the primeval forest, Bugyou Sugi failed the timber test—and lives to tell the tale.

I dismount to crawl through and around the damp, woodsy tunnel of Kuguri Sugi's titanic split trunk and tentacular branches, a fusion of melded forest trees over several generations.

Its crouching form feels gracefully posed but imperfectly balanced against my clambering limbs.

We climb higher in altitude, where I stumble on the moss-covered wood of Daio Sugi. I feel my way all around the eleven-meter circumference of its rippled trunk, treading mindfully over its tangled roots, which are gloriously sprawled across a steep slope.

The island is home to many more of these yakusugi royals, most of whom are content to remain unnamed. I envy their flamboyant symbiosis over centuries, their unapologetic way of surviving and existing in this turbulent world. I wonder if they mind my curious hands and clumsy feet, or if they are as indifferent to me as to a migrating butterfly. I want to absorb their calm composure and aloof resilience, but these millennial Cryptomeria have long since become impenetrable to humans.

We are light years away from Tokyo, where anything resembling growth is puzzle-pieced into a predictable grid. The same patriarchal clockwork that ensures the smooth operation of urban infrastructure oils the daily interactions of social harmony. It all boils down to acting according to protocol, as I remind Ryu, to saying the right thing at the right time. And behaving and responding appropriately to others requires being able to read the air, not the meteorological conditions. In such complicit social contexts, I am haplessly dyslexic.

But enough ranting about my life of living counterclockwise, being out of sync with the system, nonconforming with the consensus. Setting off into the wild and sharing my quest for transcendence through uncharted off-road cycling is my modest contribution to subverting the archipelago's insufferably harmonious society.

Are we almost there, Ryu?

By now we are rolling through dense alpine vegetation at 1,300 meters above sea level. Wet fog settles on my skin as I inhale the heavy air. This landscape is inhabited by a very different kind of stillness. Finally, Ryu slows to a stop.

Jomon Sugi is estimated to be about 7,200 years old. Its thick bark feels wrinkled and warped under my hands as I explore the gargantuan trunk's sixteen-meter circumference. Creeping upward, my fingers encounter multiple species of epiphytes growing peacefully on the ancient tree. Climbing up further, I follow the tree's twisting branches all the way to its prickly crown tipped by conifer needles.

Once upon a time, I muse, long before humans migrated to this remote island in the Pacific Ocean, this primeval cedar sprouted on the north face of Yakushima's highest mountain.

And today, Jomon Sugi is still alive, still listening, still sensing, still bearing witness to the unwritten, untold story of life and death on the island, and on the planet. A living palimpsest returned to raw bark.

I shiver as the air temperature begins to drop. Dwarfed and humbled by the yakusugi deity in front of me, I sit down on its roots and lean my back against its massive trunk. As my breathing slows to a meditative rhythm, I savor the stillness of the surrounding forest.

Jomon Sugi inhabits the Earth differently from any other living thing I have encountered before. Immovable, invincible, immortal. Its natural alchemy seems to slow the inexorable flow of time, and, with it, the torments that flood my body and mind. For the first time in a long while, I feel lightweight, lighthearted, and at peace.

I awake to the lively warble of a young uguisu, fluttering around my head before flying off into the bush. I respond with a summer melody whistled through my own ryuteki flute.

As I wrap my hands around the haptic grips of my loyal dragon bicycle, Ryu surprises me by scrolling the last dotted chapter of our pilgrimage all the way up to Jomon Sugi. *These dots are your words*, says Ryu. *Shinobu's lexicon is my living dictionary.*

Thank you, Ryu, my eternal AI ego.

I hop onto Ryu's bamboo frame and pour my renewed energy into the pulsating bike, now entirely fused into motion, music, and memories.

Let's ride, Ryu, this is just the beginning.

SHORT SHIFT
L.Y. Gu

*C*onnie jumps out of her cheap plastic chair as soon as the clock in the tiny corner of her screen displays noon.

The redder sun is streaming in through the SmartWindows, illuminating a beautiful pale teal sky over rolling orange sand dunes.

Real tempting. The SmartWindows in all the units are set to let sunlight in for ten hours a day, to reduce costs on vitamins. This has the unwanted side effect of displaying the gorgeous view outside, reminding everyone of what they can't have anymore. Not since the accident, when a SiliCone plant's waste reacted badly enough with the atmosphere that it created a toxic miasma.

Connie doesn't bother looking. She heads straight to the makeshift icebox in one corner of her unit—across from the screen and next to her bed in the other corner—and grabs the sandwich she prepared that morning. There wasn't much else around she could've cooked; space travel was expensive enough back in the day, and even though living in space became a lot cheaper for The Powers That Be to wrangle, you wouldn't know it from the prices, which hadn't changed from when you had to pay an arm and a leg to get actual bread shipped in. Only a few food staples are affordable, and even fewer can be used without a stove or an oven, which the mansions have, but the units don't get so much as a Bunsen burner. Anyway, there isn't room for one in her unit.

She finishes the sandwich in a few quick bites and paces restlessly. The cramped quarters leave her turning every few steps, which doesn't help with the restlessness. Her gaze flits over to the bike next to her screen a few times, then away, resisting.

But, if she's being honest with herself, what else is there, anyway? She could spend a week's salary on an air tank and strap it to her breathing mask, get outside for a couple hours without the miasma getting in her lungs. But then the tank would empty, and she'd be right back where she started.

She looks at the bike again.

She hates the time limit her work imposes. All teleworkers lose fifteen minutes off their clock if they're even a minute late coming back from lunch. Everyone's a teleworker these days, so it's not like they're singling her out, but it begs the question of why anyone's letting this happen. Still, it's early enough that she should be back in time.

She hops on the bike and starts pedaling. It creaks and sways—it might be needing repairs soon, or a replacement, but it's not likely to get either of those. The bikes are standard-issue from what passes for a government here: dingy and gray, cheap to manufacture, handed out to every unit to make sure everyone got their exercise while stuck indoors.

This one, though, has some decidedly nonstandard features.

She boots up the miniscreen she added a few months ago. In the beginning, she did her best to act like it wasn't a stationary bike. She set it up in front of the air vent in the wall and closed her eyes and pretended that it was a real outdoor breeze on her face instead of recycled air. But it just felt too sad.

So. The miniscreen. She saved up for it for a few months, and, when it finally arrived, she downloaded a handful of books that might be "worthwhile." Now, stir-crazy and impulsive, she gets them by the dozen—trashy romances, thrillers, anything about a world where people go about their lives without being stuck in one place forever.

The screen lights up as she pedals, a cheerful welcome message frizzing to life before dissolving to reveal a page of her latest bodice-ripper, a historical romance about two Earth residents of what they called a "city." Connie taps the screen twice and the previous line she read expands to fill the screen, scrolling at a glacial pace.

She pedals faster, and the text obligingly scrolls to match her pace, describing the coffee stains on the wooden floorboards— *wood*, what a revolutionary concept—where the protagonist's cup splattered as she stormed out following the revelation of the barista's betrayal. Faster and faster still, enough to start a slight burn in her calves as she breathes steadily, until the words are blurring past, the scene unfolding before her in ripples, the air whooshing by as she reaches terminal velocity and the bike *moves*, not in any dimension she can put a name to but zipping past her world and straight into—

There's asphalt under her wheels when she emerges, the blurry world slowly shifting back into focus around her. Connie blinks for a moment and slows her pedaling as her eyes adjust to the dimmer lighting from a single yellow sun. This sky is covered in clouds, gray and foreboding, but it's still an *open sky*, something she hasn't seen except through SmartGlass for the last seven days.

The handlebars under her hands are brown leather now, with hand brakes and speed gauges, the wheels rubber, the resistance mechanisms replaced with gears and a battery. The entire machine is something she could never have afforded on the Dris colony. Here, things are cheaper.

She slows down as much as she can, taking in the buildings to either side—quaint, faces made of brick, a material she hasn't seen except on these excursions. They're mostly little shops, but there's a kind of abundance here that still manages to surprise her. There's an *entire store* just for selling sunglasses, with a little sign out front to prove it; she stares into the windows at the rows and rows of sunglasses on racks—there can't *possibly* be enough variety to justify that.

She speeds up, enough to do a hop onto what her books called the sidewalk, and then slows again. There are people around, but not many; she veers around them easily. It still gives her a start to see people wandering outside, maskless, to smell actual fresh air. There's a hint of rain, rain that's already fallen, in the wet earth and damp streets, and rain that's about to fall, a hint of something unidentifiable in the air.

Soon, she starts to see landmarks she recognizes from the books, odd street names and traffic lights where cars loudly honk when she tries to cross. A sign in the shape of a coffee cup advertises hot wares, and she pedals toward it. Coffee is common enough on Dris, but it's the terrible generic kind, reconstituted at the molecular level into a blandly bitter powder and sold in little packets. Here, there are whole *shops* dedicated to the stuff, with names she's only ever read and never tasted—cappuccinos, lattes, mochas, and longer words she can't remember. She can't stop to try any—as soon as she stops pedaling, she'll end up back on Dris—but she breathes as deeply as she can as she passes the coffee shop, taking in the sweet aroma of medium roasts and chocolate pastries.

The bell on her bicycle starts to ring.

She barely notices at first, but it gets louder, much louder than such a small bell should be capable of. With a jolt, she remembers, and slows her pedaling.

The bike slows, then jumps back, somehow sideways from where she was. The scene around her dissolves back into a blur. The air seems to whoosh around her, and soon her surroundings crystallize back into her tiny room, seen from her perspective in the corner on her stationary exercise bike, the miniscreen dimming into power save mode.

The alarm on her work screen blares, a harsh, earsplitting buzz, and she jumps off the bike, vaulting over the front and practically falling into her seat just before the digital clock hits 12:30. With a swipe of her finger, she clocks in.

TIME TO JET

Aidan Zingler

Each massive Raliok branch extended about 0.28 kilometers outward from its main trunk. Of this distance, the last quarter had no paths or guardrails. If timed correctly, Zu could pedal hard, jump the final guardrails, and use that last bit to activate their jet thrusters. The lift would skip over the gap and drop them on the next Raliok branch. Five skips would be enough to hit the 72-A path to their destination: Oniliuk, the village that had ordered print textbooks. Sticking to the canopy meant no lower-level fauna to bother them.

Or Zu could take the longer, more winding, enclosed 71-B to 72-A through the canopy and Level 4, where no jetpack was needed. But that added 15 kilometers to what ought to be only a 13.72 kilometer journey. The lower levels beyond Level 4 held more nefarious and dangerous predators and fungi, and the sections of 71-B that dipped into Level 3 weren't fully enclosed. Both held risk, but the established paths had more of a chance for rescue if anything went wrong.

"Zu, be sensible." Karan had spot-checked the jetpack that leaned against the wall of the courier depot at the edge of the tree-city. A tuft of beard adorned his chin, his hair slicked back. "Safer to stay the *known* paths. You're going to crack a branch."

Zu adjusted the bike's brakes. "Nai, it'll go perfectly, and I'll get there with no cracked bones. If things go sour, I'll send auti fourth with a minor third. Fourth for fourth level, get it?" Regs rarely used the auti chord for reports, but the auti's heavy dissonance always delighted Zu. "You got it fueled up?"

Karan sighed. "Yai, fool. I'll be looking for that auti fourth then. And please report in regularly with the courier sefir—not your personal one this time. At least follow that reg."

"Can do." Zu shrugged on the jetpack, the straps loose around their slight frame. Karan adjusted the shoulder and belt straps until they were tight around Zu's body. "I'm going to beat the record." Zu grinned. "Picture it, Karan, my name in every textbook as the fastest courier on Vera."

Karan shook his head and checked the courier cart attachment on Zu's bike. Bits of welded polymer wrapped around the attachment with curls and curves that looked like a suffocating vine infestation. "Looks good. Be safe, Zu. Remember, there's only one of you—"

"And no other like me," Zu finished. "I'll be fine, Karan. We simulated this dozens of times. And if I succeed, maybe it'll catch on?"

"May the light not shine on that." Karan stepped back and folded his arms over his chest. "Better report in—"

"—three times a day, with a reg chord each time. I know, I know—it won't take that long. See you around, Karan!" Zu hopped on their bicycle and pedaled out of the depot's garage.

Legs pumped and the bike picked up speed. The lane curved into the 71-B, the enclosed walls a transparent dome over the path. A string of lights lined the lanes. Every 350 meters, a door or an open slot in the dome connected the path with others, but the farther from the city Zu went, the farther apart each intersection would be. Zu had calculated how far to ride in this path before jumping off and freestyling down the branch: 1,568 meters.

Zu tapped the side of their mic and sang a major third and perfect fifth set of intervals in a syncopated rhythm. The signal for a great start to the mission. The glint of lavender-hued sky, mostly hidden by the dome and canopy branches, poked its light through to leave shimmering rainbows across the dome. Beautiful day to break a record.

A few people dressed in bright colors zoomed by on their own bikes, jetboards, or katj. Zu hated the katj. Newly invented and released to the public as a hover-bike, the katj was the lumbering bear of the paths, with thrusters that blasted air downwards to keep it afloat and a beast of an engine to propel it forward. For manual bikes like Zu's, passing too close to the thrusters could easily blow a rider off-kilter. Easy to hear but annoyingly hard to avoid. One echoed from further up the path near Zu's exit, quickly approaching.

Zu navigated close to the western edge of 71-B, nearly touching the smooth enclosure's surface. The katj hurtled around the bend in the path, swerving to avoid a slower-moving bike. The driver swerved into Zu's path. No room for the jetpack, but an intersection loomed. A twist of handlebars westward into the offshoot tunnel barely missed a crash. A quick lean the other way rebalanced the bike, but Zu's momentum careened them down a barely lit path.

"Menace." Zu regained balance and cursed. This offshoot was not close to their exit point. Worse, it headed down into the lower levels of the Raliok. Jumping paths down there would mean fewer gaps to jump, but could Zu outrun the predators? The vozan, its effortless swings from leaf stem to stem, its claws and teeth dripping poison? Or the fuli, a carnivorous plant that creates webs to snare unsuspecting fools? Or the huoki with its deadly talons, poison-barb tail, and wicked beak?

Zu figured a short burst of speed from the jetpack at just the right moments ought to distance themself from the worst of the creatures. Going back to a higher level wasn't an option, too much loss in momentum. Just would have to settle for lower-level paths and thrust over their gaps. At least the gaps were much shorter in these levels.

The sunlight dimmed considerably, the dense foliage blocking its rays. The path lights shone with a blue-white glare in the growing gloom. Hisses, screeches, and wails echoed among the lower levels. The huge branches creaked a thunderous boom every few minutes, in harmony with the smack of vines and fungi tendrils against the hardwood. The wind whistled through this maze of flora. Further down, in Levels 3, 2, and 1, the silence would be broken only by the calls of fauna since the thick vegetation of Level 4 soaked up the sounds of the canopy.

Zu toggled on their headlamp and slid the headset mic closer to their mouth. The cart still rumbled behind, the books safe.

"Courier Zu Tanur in flight. Location transmitting with this update. Books still secure. Ahead of dues." The tick of the timepiece in the center of the handlebars counted down the hours and minutes Zu had to beat the records.

"Cour-set Karan Momo. Confirm location. Data puts you at Level 4—no, wait, data showing you heading downward, Level 3."

"Affirmative. Change of plans." Zu sensed the path moving downward, the air thick with pungent scents and acrid tastes. They ceased to pedal, letting the bike cruise, as they pulled a compass from their front-right vest pocket. They slapped it into its holder on the handlebars. Heading due west, slope five degrees, path below canopy and Level 4, the curl around the trunk created sharp turns every three to four thousand meters.

"Abort. Danger at maximum if you continue downward trend." Karan sang a minor triad with an auti sixth, the signal for assistance.

Zu didn't want help.

"No. I can do this. Courier Zu Tanur out." Zu hummed the five-tone encryption code to end the transmission. Zu had purposely chosen the major arpeggio to signal "no danger." A minor or acidic arpeggio would have signaled danger, but if Zu was quick to jump gaps to the next upward path, they'd not need to send any such code.

"I can do this," Zu whispered.

The enclosure opened up to the wilds of the lower levels approximately 1,500 meters ahead. Zu gripped their handlebars, pedaled hard, and mentally calculated the jump from the path to a lower branch. One was northwest and crossed over two lower branches. Further below, more branches eclipsed the lower levels so that flashes of light from glowing vines, insects, or barbed tails shone like stars in the endless twilight.

Sweat trickled down Zu's temples, the heat from Level 3 grew steadily and its air thickened the deeper Zu descended.

Closer the target branch came with each push of pedals.

Zu whistled a melodic auti-triad and swerved the bike over the path's edge the moment the enclosure ceased. The auti-triad activated the pack, and the bike and its books lifted with a howl of energy, a dizzying darkness below, before the tires hit Level 3's branch. The jets ceased. But the momentum hurled them down the pathless branch.

Zu grinned. Success! Gnarled knobs, clusters of faintly bioluminescent fungi, and rope-like vines lay scattered across the branch. Zu maneuvered around or jumped the obstacles.

The attached cargo thumped with each jump but stayed firmly attached. Up ahead, the branch split, and Zu chose the westward path that curled toward a different Raliok tree limb.

Two tapered howls came from behind. One glance, and Zu saw their worst fear—a varihok hooked onto a leaf stem, barbed prehensile tail full of poison, long and slender legs for running and jumping, and a huge snout with a leech-like mouth that sucked the blood and ligaments right out of its victims. It leapt off the stem onto the branch a good five hundred or so meters behind them.

Zu cursed and pedaled harder, their speed slowly increasing. The books bumped and rattled over the knobs and vines they raced over. The howl seared Zu's ears, the smack of talons against the branch a deadly drumbeat, and the panting—it increased in volume as the creature narrowed the distance.

This would not be their end. Only a few hundred meters away lay the gap to the next branch. Zu pushed themself harder, pedaling as fast as the bike and their muscles allowed. The book cart rattled and thumped over each gnarl of the branch.

The creature thundered closer. Another howl from Zu's left. A second varihok. Of course, they hunted in pairs.

Both were faster than Zu. There was no chance of outpedaling them, but the jetpack could increase their speed.

Zu hummed the jetpack activation for extended burn— melodic minor with a perfect octave finish. The jetpack roared to life. Slowly, too slowly, the bike lifted off the branch, their horizontal momentum pushing them up and forward. The varihok were forty meters away and closing. One spat at Zu, its venom just missing their face. It hit a vine and sizzled a hole through it.

As the bike cleared the gap and flew up along the next branch, Zu glanced behind to see the varihok leap high, swing on a leaf stem, and hit the edge of the branch. One scrambled for purchase as the other dug in with its talons.

Each book cart had an auto and manual open code. Easily sung.

Zu whistled an auti-seven arpeggio chord. A clank sounded. Zu sang it again, and the cart clanked shut. Four books hurtled down, one smacking the struggling varihok in the face, and two more slamming into the second. Both varihok screeched and tumbled into the gap. A pity Zu wouldn't beat the record with the full book haul.

Zu sang the arpeggio to shut down the jets. The bike bounced a bit but kept its forward momentum. How many more jumps to the 72-A path? Compass put them southeast. The current branch curled westward and overlapped a slightly higher branch to the northwest. That would put them closer to their destination. And further from the nightmare creatures. Zu breathed in deep and readied for another jump. Exhaustion from several kilometers of hard riding and jumping rose with Isario—the smaller moon—as sunset deepened. Isarioka, the larger moon, illuminated the semitranslucent Raliok leaves that cast huge shifting shadows along Zu's path. The last jump up into Level 4 from Level 3 had exhausted Zu's fuel but had set them onto a branch that paralleled the path they needed.

Zu checked the jetpack's gauge where it sat on their upper arm. It still read zero. The trek into Level 3 had taken too much fuel, not at all part of the plan.

Time to improvise. The path ahead paralleled the current branch but headed upward toward the enclosed dome paths.

The jump had to happen soon and fast before the domes cut off access, forcing Zu to turn around and lose all momentum.

With a twist of handlebars, Zu altered their path onto one of the stems closest to the 72-A path they needed. Narrowing toward a tapered point several hundred feet ahead, the branch swung in the evening's wind. Zu peddled hard. Muscles ached and stretched. Sweat coated Zu's brow and back. The end of the branch loomed, and the gap hung ominously like a well of swirling vegetation and howling unseen creatures.

Faster. Zu switched gears and pumped harder on the pedals, the chain screeching in protest. The tapered point curved upward, its leaf bud hanging at a sixty degree angle toward the higher branch. It ought to be enough of a ramp.

Zu leaned forward, wind whipped away sweat, and the cart clanged and shook.

The front tire hit the curve upward. Zu pulled upward. Momentum threw the bike high in an arc. The gap stretched. The moment of flight stretched like eternity. The cart creaked and groaned.

The bike's arc fell downward. For a second, the target branch seemed almost out of reach. Zu leaned even further forward, letting weight and momentum give the final push.

A slam shuddered through the entire bike and Zu's body as the bike landed right on the outer edge. The cart thudded with a low boom behind them.

Relief flooded Zu. They shifted down a gear and steered away from the looming edge. The domed section swept forward, the jump barely in time. Sound echoed in the dome louder than the grumbles of the forest proper, and the two moons shone brightly through the transparent material, both a signal of jubilation at Zu's success. With a grin, Zu tapped their mic and sang the perfect fourth followed by a major third and a perfect fifth. Signal for a perfect run. Karan likely would be shaking his head in disbelief. The last 0.45 kilometers passed quietly, the enclosed dome over the path keeping out any other murderous creatures. Exhaustion dripped through Zu's muscles.

A sign signaled the upcoming intersection for Oniliuk, the entrance path to the canopy village. This late in the evening, only the Oolio haunted the paths. The small fungoid winged creatures, their brilliant turquoise, violet, and emerald splotches shining in the light of the moons, fluttered up against the enclosures. Squishes and squelches marked the quiet in harmony with the sparse booms of the shuddering Raliok leaves, the winds quiet tonight. The path swerved around the trunk and up into the market square of the village. Situated along a thick branch, the village's green space was lined with octagonal and spherical buildings.

At the entrance to the delivery depot, the Cour-set Kava, Karan's twin, waved. Her black hair was slicked back like Karan's but cut much shorter. Zu waved back and turned wearily into the depot's path. Bits of vine and leaves clung to Zu's uniform and helmet.

"Welcome—" Kava cut off and blinked at them. "You look like you've been through hell."

"Nothing a jetpack couldn't handle." Zu came to a stop and wedged the cart into the delivery drop. "Here's the load. On time."

"Early actually! Can't believe you beat the record—" Kara flicked a switch and the books tumbled into the counter track. "Wait, why are four books missing?"

Zu grinned tiredly. "Ah, you see, varihok don't like books."

THE SLOW BOOK

Gretchin Lair

We thought we had more time.

For over a trillion trillion trillion years, watching black holes merge and explode was the only thing left to do in an empty universe.We rode ripples of spacetime like surf, the soundwaves moaning a haunting dirge. It was grueling to stay on the edge of annihilation for so long. But worse was when the black holes began to evaporate, one by one. We knew it was coming, but we still weren't ready.

When the last two black holes merged, they circled each other as closely as tango partners, their dark eyes locked, their hearts beating faster with each revolution, desperate to embrace, heedless of the cost. It was beautiful and terrible to witness.

Then we, too, were embraced.

·   ·   ·

It is blinding at first. Light is everywhere, anywhere. From the outside, black holes look opaque, unknowable. But they are bright on the inside. All the light that has ever existed in the universe churns along the edge of this black hole like letters in a book, almost all the way back to the Big Bang. Every star that has ever exploded explodes again like a flashbulb. But it's all out of order, torn pages from an infinite library. If we knew how to assemble these moments of light, we could read the entire history of the universe.

We are fortunate to be a living conscious system. When the last atoms crumbled and even protons decayed, we were forced to evolve into bodiless beings. We would not have survived in this black hole for long if we inhabited physical forms, even in a black hole the size of the entire universe.

And because matter no longer matters, we have infinite timeless time. Before, temperature was time, but space was so cold it took us ten trillion years to form a single thought. Now, our thoughts happen all at once, like overlapping echoes in a deep canyon. The clock no longer ticks. The event horizon was the past; the only future is the singularity. Until then, everything just . . . exists, both never and forever.

Until it doesn't.

•   •   •

We can no longer count years, but we can count photons, the way we used to count stars, or sheep, or the quick embers of forsaken antimatter pairs. It's difficult because the black hole has ripped everything apart so thoroughly it's like counting the ashes from a burned book. So we diligently sort through the dancing lights, attempting to bring order, shape, and form.

It is an overwhelming but soothing task. It gives us something to do when we don't know what to do. This slow, methodical pace is familiar to us.

But what began as a mechanical process becomes something more. It becomes moving. It becomes marvelous. We begin to call sorting the light "reading"; we call reassembling the light "writing." We had lost the tangible, only filling the void with our thoughts and the memory of movement. But in this space between one annihilation and the next, we are becoming unintentional librarians and unexpected authors.

•   •   •

The last book we are aware of was read by a girl in the light of a silver sun. Her book was about a bike. But the girl didn't know what a bike was any more than we did at first. How could she? Her vessel orbited an aging white dwarf, which cast only as much light as a full moon on a planet where books and bikes were plentiful.

Nothing in her book was familiar to her: not the bike, not the trees, not the blackberries. She thought the bike was riding on a fantastical ship, not a planet, because by then, planets had long been crushed to dust. Even the humans in the book were unrecognizable to her because, though she was still human, she had evolved for life in low gravity, low light, atrophy, decline. Even then, time was tedious, withering.

But the book moved her. She knew it was fragile, sacred, important. She was only thirty thousand years old, but she chose the book to be her life's work. It took her five thousand years just to learn to read it, to decipher the unfamiliar markings etched or stamped on the pages.

Though she could see in the dark, the book required light. At every opportunity, she would tuck several of her translucent limbs, some as thin as spokes, into the vessel's only viewport to read in the ashen gloom. The girl read her book over and over, a story about a bike that collected so many blackberries its basket overflowed.

Her shipmates didn't understand this behavior. They frequently reminded her of duties and activities, or encouraged her to interact with her community, or asked her to join them in the perpetual funerary songs.

The girl didn't understand it, either. All the girl knew is that when she read about the bike, it made her feel big when the ship felt small. It made her feel wild and present at the same time. It was bright when the world was dim. She could imagine the adventure. She could taste the blackberries.

She was so young but already weary of the gray corridors and somber rituals of a species preparing for extinction. The bike felt like a shining pulsar in her heart, powerful and pure.

· · ·

We wish we could speak to her now, show her what we became.

Her book was lost, as all particles were eventually lost to entropy. But she never lost the story. She never lost the bike and what it meant to her. And now we understand that every book is a beacon to those who will come after us, even if we can never imagine who they will be. We lived in darkness so long we had forgotten there was anything more. But reading about the bike, we feel things we have never experienced: the cool breeze on our hot faces, the full spectrum of golden suns, coasting downhill as swiftly and smoothly as a gravity wave, blackberries bursting warm and floral in our mouths. We remember feelings we abandoned long ago, welcoming them like old friends.

There is no reason to believe there is anything beyond the singularity. Our words will follow us into oblivion. It would be easy to believe this is all futile, easy to fall into despair.

And yet.

Everything the universe held, we hold now. As we write, everything becomes alive again, even as our event horizon fades. Neutrinos realign. Atoms bloom. The smothered stars flicker, then flare. Civilizations burble. Planets waltz. Things that were beautiful once are beautiful again.

We are learning every ending is only an evolution. We thought nothing was worse than nothing, but it turns out that even here, there is something. There is always something, even if we have to write it ourselves. For all we know, we can bring everything with us: books, bikes, the whole history of the universe. If so, this will not be the last book. It will be the first book—to be read in the universe to come.

HANG FIRE

Summer Jewel Keown

*T*hey rolled into town, all helmets and goggles and faces hidden behind cloth turned dingy from the ambient dust. Everyone was covered these days, but Margie knew they were more than ordinary travelers. She could tell from the sinewy muscles of their arms and the way they carried themselves, seemingly unaffected by the wind and surrounding dangers. Their disparate rides ranged from former racing bikes to fat-tired utility bikes to one pink Huffy with a basket still hanging on for dear life. Somehow even the Huffy looked intimidating with this crew. And there was something else about them. Almost familiar. She couldn't have explained it even if there was anyone left to explain to.

She peeked out at them from between the branches of an enormous red oak, high above the ground, careful to hide herself behind the now-withered leaves of the great old tree. No one had been here in . . . what had it been now, at least a month? She'd started to lose count of the days. Everyone she could have considered family was long gone: her aunt and uncle who had taken her in but whose house was already too full, her few friends who had disappeared one by one into the thick dust of the horizon. She almost regretted staying behind when the last group packed up what they could carry and started their trek out to find a place they might trade work for water and food. Wherever that might be, if that place even still existed.

Staying was foolish. The dust had ruined everything here. Still, Margie had known she needed to. She just didn't know why. She couldn't explain it but she knew: the waiting wasn't just entropy, it had a purpose. Eventually, she would figure out what it was, or she would die figuring. All she knew was that it wasn't yet time to go. Her bones had told her that, though it seemed foolish at best. So she had watched them leave, the last people in the world she had any ties to, and then she had survived. Mostly.

The crew stopped and gathered in a circle just far enough from her that she couldn't hear what they said. She'd always considered herself a loner, but she'd learned the true meaning of loneliness this past month. It was an actual physical ache, that lack of people, and now here they were: real, probably-not-hallucinatory people. Margie found herself leaning toward them like a tree stretching toward sunlight and rain, contorting itself with the effort. She closed her eyes and breathed in the hum of their unintelligible words. It sounded like the home she'd never had.

Lost in the murmuration, Margie inched forward on her branch, then leaned a little more. It wasn't until she heard the crack that her eyes shot open and she tried to scramble back. Too late—the branch propelled gravity-down, with her riding shotgun. She hit the ground and went into a tumble to break the impact, ignoring the pain radiating from her shoulder. She jumped to her feet, ready to run.

The crew was faster. Before she could dash, she was surrounded. They stood between her and any measure of safety, but she wasn't ready to give up. They held kitchen knives, an axe, a short camping shovel. Weapons as motley as their rides. In her peripherals, Margie measured them against her knowledge of her own strength and speed, and she chose the smallest of the figures, the one holding some kind of a rubber mallet. The way they held it told her they'd probably never wielded it in a fight.

She spun around and charged toward them, bracing for impact. Shoulder-checking the person, pain shot back through her shoulder again; she ignored it. The impact sent them both sprawling, and Margie put all the fuel she had into a run. They were not going to catch her, to do . . . whatever crews like these did. She'd heard stories.

Adrenaline pushed her feet to move faster while her stomach growled, warning her that she didn't have much in her. Any moment they would lay chase. She didn't know how long she could outrun them. She heard the crew moving behind her, but all at once, they stopped.

"Let her go," she heard one of the figures say. A softer voice than she'd expected, though firm underneath, with notes of kindness that Margie was probably imagining. "We know her. She won't harm us. And she will come back. It is written."

Margie kept running, ignoring the nonsense words. What did that mean, "We know her"? These people might feel kind of familiar in a weird way, but she knew they'd never met before. She wasn't going to fall for whatever their tactic was. No way was she going to come back, though. She wasn't a fool. Even with everything, she wasn't ready to die.

There was an old water tower, not too far from the center of town. Empty for years, of course, and half rusted out. Margie climbed it and crouched on the metal walkway, stories above ground, exposed to the elements but at least able to keep watch. She kept an eye on the crew as they investigated the skeletons of the few houses and shops that hadn't been burned or collapsed. Good luck to them. Any good supplies had been picked over long ago. She knew, she'd been picking the last month and found very little. What she had found, she'd hidden well. At least, she hoped.

Her adrenaline now spent, a tired ache permeated her entire body. She knew better than to sleep, but it was coming and would brook no refusal.

It was dusk when she came back to herself. She stifled a groan as she adjusted herself on the metal platform. Her stomach protested its emptiness, and she silently told it to please just shut up.

The beginnings of a fire flickered in the distance. She squinted at it. The crew must be making camp for the night. They were smart to stay out in the open. The houses could be tempting, but their foundations were weak, and sleeping inside wasn't worth the gamble. She'd been in the basement of an old church during a storm when the building fell on top of her. She hadn't been sure if she'd make it out of the rubble, and when she finally clawed her way out, she'd learned that lesson well.

Her stomach growled again, an angry, persistent wolf tearing at her insides. A foolish thought struck her. Surely the crew had some food stores. Perhaps if she waited until full night, she could sneak in and grab some provisions while they slept. She knew it was unwise, possibly suicidal, but so was thinking she was going to survive much longer without something in her belly besides leaves and the few questionable mushrooms she'd found.

When it was dark enough not to be seen, she crept carefully down from the tower. As she tested each rung to see if its rust would give way beneath her foot, she wondered what it had been like when this structure had held enough water in it to just . . . sit there. Just waiting for a time it would be needed. Extra. What would it have been like to immerse herself in that water, head to toe, letting it wash over her? There was a memory, deep within her, of swimming. A lake, maybe, or a pond. Water just there, unguarded, free. Now it felt like a ridiculous fever dream.

Touching ground, Margie stopped and listened. The winds were blessedly light tonight, and she could breathe without a cloth barrier. That was rare anymore.

The moon was out more than she would have liked. Darkness would have been to her advantage, but she would work with what she had. She would wait until they slept, watch for them to leave a gap in their vigilance, then be in and out quickly.

There was a gap under one of the porches around the corner from where the crew had set up camp. Margie had hidden from a dust storm there one day when she'd been out scavenging. She crept into it now. From here she could hear them, at least somewhat. She strained to make out words. They were indistinct, but one thing she did hear was . . . laughter.

It was real laughter, she could tell, even from her hiding spot. Almost . . . happy? Was that even possible? It wasn't the kind of laughter that comes from gallows humor and bitterness, the kind that helps you get through the worst. This was different, and it cracked open something inside her. Out of nowhere, she felt an urge to run toward the laughter, to drink it in.

From her vantage point, with the moon's annoyingly bright light, she could see the crew huddled around the fire. They were unwrapped now, their faces exposed to the night sky. She couldn't make out their features, but she imagined they were smiling. She tested her own face, tugged the corners of her mouth up, held the now-unfamiliar expression in place.

A loud crack sounded in the distance, stirring the crew into action. Their laughter stopped and each one reached for whatever weapon lay within arm's length. The crew conferred, using hand signals to decide who would stay and who would go.

Margie wanted to laugh. She knew what the sound was. It happened every few days. Another building shedding its skin, roofing cracking apart, walls falling. From the direction the sound came, she guessed it was the library. She'd already scavenged what she wanted from there, a few books that hadn't been destroyed by dust and heat and exposure from the holes in the roof. Old folktales and histories. They were hidden away with her other finds now.

Only two of the crew remained around the fire. Her odds were improving. If she'd believed in fate . . . but she didn't. No one did, not anymore. That was the stuff of the old tales in books. One of the remaining people sat next to the fire, their back to her. Their silhouette reminded her of a drawing in one of those books. She shrugged off the inconvenient recollection.

The seated figure gestured to the standing one, who bent down beside them, their ear cocked to listen. Margie couldn't hear what they were saying, but she knew this was about the best chance she was going to get. There was a pouch next to the fire. Surely it held food. Her stomach rumbled in anticipation.

She started to creep, slowly and carefully, out from underneath the porch. She wasn't sure if she had it in her to outrun them, fight them if needed. Two to one was not great odds, but if she was going to do this, she had to do it now.

As she took in some deep breaths, steadying herself, the second figure stood, then began walking in the direction the others had run before. Surely she wasn't going to get this lucky. There was always a catch. And yet, she had to try.

Margie sunk into a crouch, glancing from side to side. No time like the *Now!* She sprinted toward the fire, dust kicking up at her heels. Gone was the cover of the old house, she was out in the open now. The seated figure hadn't moved yet. Could they hear her? Surely her steps were echoing in the night, but she could only hear her own heartbeat.

In moments she was there, reaching her hand out to grab the bag. She braced herself. There was no way this person was going to let it go without a fight. *Don't question it, just go.* But she couldn't stop herself, she turned to look.

A woman sat, crossed-legged, gazing up at her. She looked young, in her midtwenties possibly, dark brown eyes reflecting the fire's flame. Margie snatched the bag to her chest with one hand, formed her other hand into a fist.

The woman smiled at her. Smiled! Margie didn't know how to react. Was this a trick? Were the others laying in wait for her? She swiveled her head around, searching for any peripheral motion, but it was just the two of them, caught in a moment under the moon. Margie felt tempted to stay, to say . . . something.

What was she doing? She shook off the moment, gripped the bag tighter, and darted toward the far shadows. She turned behind a row of half-collapsed houses, waiting for the chase. But there was nothing. Still, the others would soon return and she ran for blocks until her legs gave out. An old gas station waited on the corner, its shelves long emptied. She yanked the doors open and headed into one corner. Just enough light came through the splintered windows for her to see the bag.

She dumped it out, hungrily sorting through the items inside. Some bike tools, which she set next to her. Perhaps she could finally fix up the old mountain bike she'd found and hidden a couple weeks ago. A lighter. That would be useful. The crew was definitely going to miss this bag, but she couldn't worry about them.

Her hands closed on a metal travel mug. She shook it, and the liquid inside it jiggled. Margie spun open its top and sniffed. Water. She took it to her mouth, greedily chugging it down.

It tasted a little off, with the tinge of chemicals in all water anymore, but it was heaven in liquid form. She nearly cried.

And there was food too. Not a bounty, but enough. A small pouch held some nuts. Margie forced herself to eat them slowly, lest she trigger her empty stomach to bring them back up again. She savored every bite, ran her tongue across their ridges and smooth parts, closed her eyes against the earthy flavor. Some dandelions wrapped in cloth. Not her favorite, she'd scavenged dandelions so many times, but it was food and that made it glorious. She set them aside and continued investigating the bag.

A cloth wrapped around a heavier item. She unwound it carefully. It could be anything. A weapon, something to trade . . . a . . . book? Seriously? She pulled the cloth from the book and held it in her lap. Its cover was worn, its pages pliant. In the dim light she opened its cover and squinted inside. It was full of handwritten words, drawings she could barely see.

She moved closer to the window. Safety be damned, she wanted to know what this crew was carrying around with them. What was so important?

Moonlight was slowly giving way to that hint of predawn sky, and she had to squint. She could just make out the words: "As we journey, we collect our family. The road winds and leads us to the lost ones who will become the found ones."

She gulped. It was like she had read these words before, but she knew that she hadn't. "At the end of the road we will build our new community. We will heal what has been wounded. We will make a home to bring in the new days to come."

What was this book? A journal? A guide? A bible? She paged through it more.

She stopped at a drawing that looked familiar. It was the woman by the fire, seated just as she had been. "Welcome," was written just below her figure.

Feelings began to stir in her, ones she'd forgotten the names for it had been so long. She had never known what it was to be welcome. The ache took hold of her, spoke of all she'd always wished for. Family. Community. Home.

She shook herself. *Stop it*, she commanded, *this thinking is dangerous*, but the hope was already blooming. Where she thought she was barren, there was some meager soil after all, and the seed of the word *Welcome* was sending out tiny tendrils, rooting. She knew better. Who were those people out there? They would likely sooner kill her than speak to her. As though they wanted another body to feed.

The later pages of the book were still blank. She turned to the last page with writing on it, and she stopped.

The figure was crudely drawn, but it was her. Her crooked nose, the scar on her left temple, her curly hair tied off to one side. She was astride a bicycle, one she knew. The mountain bike she had hidden. How . . . how could they possibly know?

Two halves of her fought each other, practicality and hope, survival and foolishness. She's made it this long listening to something she couldn't explain, but trust wasn't something anyone could afford anymore. Certainly not her. Certainly not. . . . Except she already knew what she was going to do. Whether it was the right thing or the thing that might get her killed.

Stuffing the book back in its bag, along with the bike tools, the fabric, and the other parcels, Margie stood. She pulled open the door and launched herself out into the open. All the months of self-preservation gave way to a single-minded impulse, and she ran for her hiding place.

When she reached the half-collapsed garage, Margie carefully maneuvered herself between broken boards, feeling her way in the darkened interior. In the very back, behind sheets of cracked plywood, were her paltry supplies. Some holey blankets she'd been saving for winter, a screwdriver, empty plastic water bottles, a backpack, and other things she'd thought could be useful someday. And behind it all, the mountain bike. She'd found it in decent condition after the first few waves of people left town, back before everyone had been watching their own backs for the smallest scrap. Someone had left it locked up to a bike rack. All it took was an old saw and a lot of time to get it free. She wasn't ready to go anywhere then, but she'd thought a bike could be useful someday. Whether it was luck or fate, she would bring it out today.

It took some time to tug it free of the garage, but she leaned it against one standing wall and looked it over in the morning's creeping light. From her stolen bag she took out the tools and went to work, tightening bolts, airing up tires. She even had a few spare tubes she'd stolen from a looted bike shop. Whether they were the right kind for this bike or not, she could make an offering of them.

She threw a leg over the frame and pushed off. The bike rode just fine, miracle of miracles. Quickly, she gathered up the stolen bag and filled her backpack with as much of her hidden supplies as she could carry, throwing it over her shoulders. Then she began to ride.

As she pedaled, she had an awful thought: What if they had already moved on? What if they had left with the morning light? After all, she'd stolen from them, perhaps they were cautious that there were others here that might harm them.

She knew nothing about these people. She knew that she could be riding into a fight, that they could strip her of all her supplies and leave her bleeding, or worse. But she had to try. And surely, that drawing must mean something.

Turning the corner toward where the crew had set up camp, she gasped. They were lined up, facing her, each holding or astride their bike. They were packed up and ready to go.

Margie stopped, just feet from them, and waited. The woman from last night, the one who had been seated by the fire, who had put up no fight when she'd stolen from her and ran, stepped forward.

"We've been waiting," she said. "Are you ready to go?"

Margie nodded. The words would not come. She had been waiting too, and it was time. Wherever they were going, she would, too, until the very end.

THE OPAL'S DAWN

Mariah Southworth

*T*he last escape pod left the scanner's range just before a hellish crackle bubbled up from the depths of the control module. All across the access panel, lights flashed red before going dark. Captain Hazel Carter slammed a hand down on the side of the machine. "Damn," she hissed. With a sinking apathy, she realized that it didn't matter that she could no longer use the terminal. She had managed to divert enough power to the launch system and shielding for everyone else to evacuate, but it had taken everything the ship could give. There was no way she could escape. She could manually drain the systems one at a time to cool the core temporarily, but that would only delay the inevitable explosion.

The only thing left to do was go down with the ship.

Hazel straightened and looked around the empty bridge, with its cracked screens, abandoned chairs, and fallen coffee cups. A patch of blood, brilliant red against the stark white floor, lay spattered in the corner, though when or how someone had gotten hurt she didn't know.

The adrenaline that had gotten her this far suddenly abandoned her, leaving her bone-weary. She drifted over to her command chair, fingers trailing over the sleek leather armrest. It had taken so much work to get here, and so many people had thought she hadn't deserved it.

Well, this at least would prove them wrong. Pity she wouldn't be around to gloat. Hazel lowered herself into the chair with a sigh and closed her eyes.

"Excuse me?"

Hazel jumped, startled, and stared at the unexpected and inexplicable stranger standing in front of her, an old fashioned bicycle propped up beside her on a kickstand.

Oh great, the captain thought. *Near-death is making me hallucinate.*

There could be no other explanation for the slim, tawny-skinned young woman with the shaved head and notably Egyptian-esque eye makeup. She wore tight pants and a crop jacket over a silver tank top, and a wide, sparkling smile stretched across her face.

"Hi," she said brightly. "You're Hazel Carter, right?"

"I . . ." Hazel managed to croak past her surprise. "Uh . . . yes?"

"Oh good, good!" the stranger bubbled. "Hello! My name's Magdalene, and I am *such* a huge fan!" She pulled a book out of her jacket pocket, a real book, like something out of a museum, with paper and everything. The girl stepped away from her bicycle, flipping to a blank page in the book and unclipping a pen from its side. "Could I maybe get your autograph?" she asked hopefully, holding out the book and pen.

Hazel stared at her. "Uh . . ."

Magdalene's smile faltered, and her eyes flicked around the room. She finally seemed to realize the state of the bridge. "Oh!" she exclaimed, withdrawing. "Oh no. This isn't a good time, is it?" She winced and stepped back towards the bicycle. "I should go."

"Wait!" Hazel burst, her shock finally dropping from her. This was no hallucination! This was real! Everyone should have gotten out, damn it! All of that adrenaline came rushing back now that she knew there was someone who still needed saving.

"It's alright," Magdalene assured her, as if she *wasn't* on the bridge of an exploding starship. "I can come back."

"There isn't going to be a back!" Hazel yelled, jerking out of her command chair. "We're going to die here, you . . . you . . ." She looked from the girl to the bicycle and back. "How did you even get here? I thought everyone evacuated!"

"Die?" The girl's eyes widened, but she seemed more incredulous than scared. "No, no, no, no.

Look at you! You're too young to die." She laughed.

"I mean, that's my sentiment," Hazel said, confusion warring with panic.

"No, you don't understand. This is . . ." Magdalene trailed off, looking around the room again.

"Where is this? Oh!" Her eyes lit up. "This is the ship!" She flipped to a different page of her book, and now Hazel could see that there was script printed across some of the pages. "It is, isn't it? This is the *Opal's Dawn*!" She looked back up at Hazel, wide eyes glittering. "Oh, and you don't have a way out?" she breathed, awestruck.

"No!" Hazel snapped, the absurdity of the situation sapping her minimal patience.

"You're really going to explode?"

"Yes!"

"Oh. Oh my." Magdalene tucked her book and pen away. "I never thought . . . but you never *did* tell anyone how you escaped. Oh my goodness!" She beamed and hopped back onto her bike. She patted the seat behind her, which Hazel could now see was large enough for two, unlike a normal bike's. Actually, there was quite a bit off about the bicycle. The wheels were made of metal, and the frame was painted with a matte black that seemed to suck at the light of the room. A glass orb sat nestled between the handlebars and the front wheel.

"What?" Hazel asked.

"Well, get on," Magdalene told her.

Hazel looked around the room, glared at the dead control panel, and then shrugged. She was going to die anyway. The captain climbed onto the bike and wrapped her arms around the stranger's waist.

"Here we go!" Magdalene said brightly. She kicked back her stand, placed her feet on the pedals, and squeezed the gears. Hazel gasped as brilliant rainbow light flashed to life from the front of the bicycle. She instinctively tightened her grip as Magdalene surged forward. For a brief moment, the wall of the bridge rushed towards them . . . and then it was gone. Dark blue void domed around them, and when Hazel looked down, she saw a translucent silver road whizzing by beneath their wheels, lights sparking off as it appeared and disappeared a few feet before and behind the bicycle.

Magdalene shot her a smile over her shoulder.

I'm dead, Hazel thought, mouth gaping open. Then she realized that was ridiculous and gave herself a firm shake. "Are you an alien?" she demanded.

"Oh no, no." Magdalene laughed, then looked thoughtful. "Well . . . I mean, we're still *called* humans. I'm from the future."

Hazel raised an eyebrow. "The future," she said flatly.

"Yes!" She grinned widely, her teeth pearl white against her skin. "My great-great-grandmother actually went to one of your lectures on deep space exploration. Of course you haven't *made* that speech yet, but you looked amazing! She took a picture with you and everything."

Hazel paused to process this. "You have a bicycle."

"Time machine," Magdalene corrected.

That . . . was no more or less weird than anything else. "And a book," she pressed.

"Yes."

"Books haven't looked like that since what, a hundred years?"

"They came back into style," she said brightly.

"This is . . ." Hazel looked around at the void, the silver road, the *bicycle*. "I can't believe this."

Magdalene looked suddenly worried. "You really mustn't tell anyone."

Hazel barked out a laugh. "Who would believe me? *I* don't believe me."

"I mean, I *know* you won't tell anyone because I'm from the future and you never did," she said, frown deepening, as if she was just working this out as she said it. "But still . . . I would get in an awful lot of trouble if anyone found out I interfered." She gave Hazel a chagrined look. "I'm just such a *big* fan, you know. I'm visiting all of them—all the women in history who inspired me." She took one hand off the handlebars and briefly patted the bulge her book made in her jacket pocket before going back to steering.

Hazel frowned as the implications of this caught up with her. "And . . . wait, really? Me?"

"Oh course!" Magdalene exclaimed, her enthusiasm making the bicycle wobble alarmingly. "The first woman to fly faster than light! The hero of *Opal's Dawn*! The founder of the Gemspark Association!"

"The *what* association?" Hazel asked sharply.

"Oh! Uh, um." Magdalene winced. "Nothing, forget I said anything."

It hasn't happened yet, Hazel thought, remembering Magdalene's book. *She has a history book. I'm in a history book, and there's more that I'm going to do. I really am going to live past this . . . and Magdalene knows more about me than I do.*

Hazel couldn't decide if that was amazing or unsettling. Maybe it was both. They rode in silence for a time, Magdalene gently pedaling along. Hazel wondered if she really *needed* to pedal, and, on that note, if they were going anywhere at all, or if the future fangirl was just stalling for time while she figured out what she was going to do.

There was a whole *future* out there, one that Hazel might not ever get to see . . . if she even wanted to see it. *Could* she see it? Could Magdalene take her there? Did she even *want* to know? There would be good things, certainly, but probably bad as well, and humanity had produced plenty of stories about the tragedy of knowing what was coming and being unable to stop it.

"So, um. Thank you," Hazel said, breaking the silence. "For saving me."

Magdalene glanced back at her, startled. "I . . . oh, I guess I did, didn't I?" Hazel almost laughed at the baffled look on Magdalene's face. She didn't though. No sense in embarrassing her rescuer.

"Do you still want that autograph?" she asked.

"Oh, would you?" Magdalene brightened and groped for her book. "Please!" She pulled it out and quickly passed it back to Hazel before grabbing the handlebars again.

The book felt unexpectedly heavy in Hazel's hands. She had never held one before. In her time, all they had were holodisks and readers. What future history was held here on these anachronistic pages? She could find out anything she wanted. About her life, about the future.

Hazel very determinedly opened the book to the part where she remembered the pages being blank. She unclipped the pen and signed her name, then stuffed the thing back into Magdalene's jacket. Magdalene gave her another of her dazzling smiles.

Hazel settled back, feeling suddenly tired. "So, what now?" she asked wearily.

"Well, that cruiser *Her Dark Mien* picks you up . . . tomorrow, I suppose." Magdalene cocked her head thoughtfully. "Heh, time travel, am I right? Anyway, they find you on a mining asteroid base that you hacked into to broadcast a distress call."

Hazel nodded. "Alright," she said. She really could tell no one . . . no one would ever believe her. Hell, give it a few years and she might start to think she had made the whole thing up.

"But . . . um, well . . . if you *wanted* . . ." Magdalene trailed off and gave her a pointed look. Hazel, unable to discern her meaning, just frowned. Magdalene blushed, looking embarrassed. "I mean . . . time machine," she said.

Hazel stared a moment. "Oh!" she exclaimed. She had already dismissed the future as a possibility, but the past . . .

Magdalene beamed excitedly at her. "Right?"

"You know," Hazel said slowly, a smile spreading over her face. "I've always wanted to meet Cleopatra."

FALLING

Annie Carl

I'm in the back seat of a bike cab heading for the Edmonds train station. It isn't too far from my house, just two miles past my bookstore that Dad will be watching for a week.

The cabbie pulls up to the drop-off curb and unloads my small rolling bag. I slide ungracefully off of the bench, ankles wobbling beneath me as I settle my weight on them. I run my wrist over the cabbie's wrist to pay them for the ride and turn to face the station.

Nerves twinging in my midsection, I nearly tip over as I try to sit down on a bench. Cheeks burning, I manage to get myself seated.

How could I possibly learn how to ride a bike? It hasn't worked out before. My balance is shit, my legs are weak, and how am I supposed to stay upright?

A conductor calls the train as it pulls up in front of me, still smelling a bit like the diesel it used to run on. An attendant stands just inside, scanning wrists for ticket information. They watch me pull myself aboard, raising an eyebrow at the conductor.

"Thank you for riding the Coast Starlight today," they say as their ticket scanner chirps.

"Thanks," I mutter, grabbing my suitcase.

"Are there really disabled people, still?" I hear the attendant whisper to the conductor. Glancing back, I see the conductor shrug and lean over to whisper a response.

Ugh. Not every parent decides to genetically alter their baby.

Settling myself in my window seat, I glance at the other side of the car. The windows there look out on the glorious Puget Sound, shining in the spring sun. I grin at a little girl sitting across from me. She smiles back. The car lurches forward as the train sets into motion. I pull the new Melissa Chambers book out of my backpack, flipping to my spot.

The train is nearing downtown Seattle. I set my book down and inhale. Seattle has changed dramatically since the West Coast State Coalition secession. Plants drip down the sides of skyscrapers, moss grows in fluffy clumps along guardrails and concrete walls and brick facades. Plantlife in the WCSC has never been happier during human colonization.

The citizens of the WCSC agreed to sell their cars when the West Coast states seceded from the United States. Which means we all get around via walking, scooters, skates, biking, or bike cabs. Disabled people get special dispensation to keep their cars, so I could have kept mine. I didn't, but it turns out that taking bike cabs everywhere is expensive. So now I need to learn to ride a bike. The WCSC provides free bike lessons, so I signed up.

Setting my book down, I pull my tablet out of the side pocket on my backpack. I run my fingers along one side and it unlocks, stretching an onion skin–thin piece of processing chip between the two fingerholds.

"Call the store," I order at the background of my cat Rosco. The screen blanks out, then reforms around Dad's face.

"Earthbound Books, this is Jasper speaking." His face brightens from professional seriousness to delight when he sees it's me. "Bean! Are you there yet?"

"No, Dad." I giggle, nerves flooding my bloodstream. "I'm on the train still. I wanted to call and see how things're going at the shop."

"They're fine. I totally know what I'm doing." Dad's goofy smile soothes my heart. He glances at something beyond my screen. "I'll be right with you folx. Just on the phone with the proprietress."

"Go, Dad," I stage whisper. "You know how to reach me. Love you."

"I love you back, Bean," he says, grinning up at me.

The almost four-hour trip passes in a series of chapters read and landscape observed.

The train slows as we come into Tacoma. The city is dripping in green, dewdrops and rain adding an extra sparkling gleam to the buildings. The station itself is open air and covered in draping ivy and morning glories.

I stumble off the train, backpack slung over one shoulder, suitcase handle in my other hand. Scattered, I nearly trip over myself as I enter the Tacoma station. I sit on the first bench I see, taking a deep breath and working to get my shaking hands under control. Tripping is a regular part of my life, but the adrenaline surge at almost falling never ceases.

After a few minutes, my body is back to its normal wobbly self. Joints stiff, I carefully adjust my backpack and grab the handle of my suitcase.

I take another deep breath and make my way with tenuous balance to the waist-high kiosk sticking up from the floor. It chirps and rises slightly out of the ground. A pleasant automated voice comes from a speaker set in the slanted top.

"Welcome," it chimes. "Please swipe your wrist and then insert your tablet."

I fumble my tablet out of my backpack.

"Thank you, Mx. Amberson," it says. "Have a lovely evening. Your first bicycling class is at 8:30 a.m. Do make an effort to be on time. A bike cab has been called for you. It will meet you at the south exit in five minutes."

I find my way to the exit, and a cab is waiting for me. The tall cyclist helps me load up the cab and takes off, away from the train station.

The WCSC bike classes are in a gigantic, one-story, circular building. Pulling my tablet out, I look up the coordinates as the cabbie pulls up to an entrance. The building is laid out like a multicolored wagon wheel with three connected circles and a central, rainbow hub.

"Thanks," I mumble at the cabbie as I practically fall out of the cab, suitcase and pack tumbling behind me. Righting myself, I run my wrist over theirs and stand, staring at the wall of the building. It is covered in all manner of blue-green plant life.

I manage to make my way to the proper hallway and room. Holding my wrist up to the door, it slides into the wall, and I have just enough time to enter before it whooshes closed, nearly clipping me in the butt. My butt barely clears the doorway.

The room itself is sparse but comfortable. I hang my clothes up in the closet, medical supplies on the tiny bathroom counter, and stack the three Melissa Chambers books on the small nightstand along with my tablet in its charger.

Sitting on the squishy bed, I look around the minimalist room again. Exhaustion hits me in a clattering, eye-drooping wave, and I force myself to stand. I have three days of bike classes before I head home. I want to make the most of my downtime and explore the WCSC building. And, as tired as I am from the trip, my stomach is gurgling with impatience for food.

Yanking my tablet out of the charger and grabbing a book, I stuff both in my backpack and force myself to lumber out of the room.

Double-checking which level has food available, I toggle the elevator switch. Once there, I circle the stalls and shops, marveling at the food. I find a traditional ramen stand and sigh happily.

"One ramen with the works, please." I smile at the older woman running the stand and swipe my wrist over her reader.

I settle at a table and smile at a woman who looks about my age as she walks by with a tray. She's beautiful and stops when I smile.

"Can I sit here?" she asks. My stomach goes a bit wobbly at her words.

"Yes," I murmur.

She sits and notices the book I'm pulling out of my bag.

"Is that the new Melissa Chambers book?" she asks, words husky and excited. She tugs at one of the box braids hanging over her shoulder.

I light inside.

"It is!" Nerves completely gone, I shove the book across the table. "Have you read it yet?"

"I haven't." She does a little wiggle-shiver movement as she reverently touches the spine and picks up the book. "I didn't think it was available yet."

"It's not." I smile sheepishly at her. "But I own a bookstore and get access to books earlier than my customers."

Before she can answer someone across the food court calls "Stef!" and she spins to wave.

"Gotta go," she says, turning back to me and flashing a brilliant smile. Before I can say anything else, she's gone.

•　　•　　•

The alarm goes off with a cheerful chirp far too early the next morning. I step muzzily into the shower, my brain insisting I haven't had enough sleep.

I throw on a pair of jeans, T-shirt, and cozy sweater. I tie my slightly curly hair back in a ponytail and stare at myself in the mirror for a second, taking in all of the bumpy curves and soft planes. Except for my underdeveloped calves. Those will always be stick-straight.

Nodding, I try on a "let's be friendly while we crash our bikes into each other" smile. It sort of hitches at one side, and I sigh.

"Let's get this over with so I can go home," I grumble at my reflection. Nodding once more, I leave the washroom, scoop up my backpack, book, and tablet, and follow the directions to the recreation level of the hub's core.

Stepping out of the lift, I can see into some of the rooms along the curved hallway. One holds an enormous swimming area, with a real sandy beach at one end and an olympic sized pool at the other. Hot tubs, salt water pools, and shallower tubs are scattered in the space between the beach and pool. Continuing down the hall, I observe gyms, grassy fields, turf fields, dance studios, and tracks. I stop in front of a door with a neat sign next to it reading Bicycle Track. I swipe my wrist and walk into the room.

A track loops the domed space. Windows on either side of the oval show the rooms to either side, but I'm too busy marveling at the size of the bike track to notice. I gawk at the four bikes lined up by the door, perfectly balanced. The track itself has six lanes made out of some kind of hard surface. Falling on it will hurt.

I set my backpack in a cubby by the door and step farther into the room, stumbling over my own feet a bit as I take everything in.

Over the next few minutes, four other people arrive at the bike track. The final and fifth person is the woman from the food court. Gods that body. And with her hair. My knees have that hollow feeling.

"Hello, everyone." Words come out of their mouth and I try to focus on them. My middle trembles, and I worry that if I try to move, I will fall flat on my face. "I'm Stef Reese, she/they, your instructor for the next few days. I also work at a frame shop just outside of Tacoma. If you ever need a custom bike, just look up Framing and Spoke. Bikes are basically my life." Stef smiles, and I grin in response. "For the next three days we're here to learn how to ride bikes. Let's get to know each other before we start skinning knees."

My knees twinge at her words.

She leads the way toward the middle of the track. I follow at the back in case I really do fall flat on my face. We all sit on the turf in the center of the track, knee-to-knee, and look to Stef.

She nods at the older man next to her. "I'm Frank Bowman, he/him," he says, nodding his head at each of us. "I had a knee replaced recently and thought this would be a great way to get back on the horse. Bike."

We all laugh.

"I'm Henrietta Bowman, she/they." Henrietta turns loving eyes on Frank. "In 38 years of marriage, we've been apart only a few times. So I decided it was high time to learn how to ride a bike."

Smiling, Stef looks at the next person in the small circle we present. That person is me. She's looking at me!

"Uh, hi." My mouth trips over the word, heart slamming into my ribs. Heat races into my face, and not just because Stef is watching. Everyone else is too. "I'm Jordyn Amberson, she/her. I never learned how to ride a bike because . . ." Trailing off, I gesture to my lower body. "It wasn't something that came easily, I guess. But I need to get to my bookstore every day, and bike cabs are expensive. Walking isn't really an option. So here I am."

"Here you are, indeed." Stef smiles deep into my gaze.

How the fuck am I supposed to learn something with those gorgeous amber eyes watching me?

". . . Louis George, they/them." I tune in to Louis speaking, though I can hardly hear them over the thumping of my pulse. "You all can call me Georgie if you like. I'm used to walking everywhere, but some places are too far to walk. Thought I'd give a bike a try."

We all nod at each other, smiling in varying degrees of shyness.

Stef tells us each to choose a bike. I pick one on the outside, pluck the helmet off the seat, and lift my right leg to swing it over the seat. Stumbling, my foot barely clears the frame. Georgie takes the bike next to mine, with Frank and Henrietta on their other side.

On tippy toes, I balance enough to quickly jam the helmet on. The bike begins to lower, and I almost fall again. It stops once my feet are flat on the ground.

"Alright let's get started," Stef calls, her voice carrying well through the track area. "You'll notice your bikes have all lowered so your feet are on the ground. That's fine, we'll start scooting around so you can get a feel for your bike. Make sure those helmets are buckled, not just on your heads."

My seat is comfortable, and the handlebars are not too far away. Pressing down, I work my legs and feet against the ground. Losing my balance, I overcorrect and fall to my right, balance and weak legs working against me catching myself. In the moment before landing, I try to curl into a ball. I land on my side on the metallic track.

Georgie, Frank, and Henrietta are already ahead of me, though Frank has fallen off his bicycle too. Wincing, he stands and gets back on.

"Fuck," I exhale, winded. "Ouch."

"You'll probably have some bruises tomorrow," Stef says, coming over to me. "But they won't be too bad. Come on, let's get you back up."

She helps me stand, and I awkwardly swing my leg back over the bike. My foot gets tangled with the frame, and I almost fall again.

"It looked like you weren't really making much progress." Stef leans over the handlebars, and I quiver with how close she is. "Just keep focusing on scooting yourself forward. You'll find your balance in no time."

"Thanks," I whisper, smiling at her. She grins back.

The rest of the morning was one big Jordyn-falls-off-the-bike lesson. I can't stay on for more than a few minutes before overbalancing and crashing to the ground. By the time the call for lunch comes, I'm aching and never want to see another bicycle again.

Stef's beautiful face pinches as she watches me grab my backpack and follow the others to the food level.

During weight training, I'm assigned leg exercises.

"I really don't know how this is going to help," I mumble as I complete my tenth squat. I have to do them with my palms against the wall so I don't lose my balance.

"I'm honestly not sure either," Stef says as she comes up behind me. Smiling uncertainly, she takes my hand, helping me gain some balance as I shift to standing. I shiver at the tingles going up my arm. "I've never had a student quite like you. Let's see what we can do over the next two days."

By the final day, I'm sitting against the wall, alternately reading and watching as Frank, Henrietta, and Georgie all pedal gracefully around the track. I've made it through my stack of Marissa Chambers, reading the first book twice. After my 27th fall that left a bruise dark as a thundercloud, Stef wouldn't let me back on a bike.

Twenty-seven falls in three days. I rub my hand over my face and work hard against the lump in my throat. I swore to myself I wouldn't cry while I cheered on my friends.

Despite living all over the WCSC, Frank, Henrietta, Georgie, and I have become close during our biking endeavors. We all trade tablet information and promise to stay in touch.

My three new friends mount their government-issue training bikes for the last time. I can't focus on them, memories from the night before still fresh in my mind.

"Do you have a book-loving boyfriend back home?" Stef had asked me during my last night at the hub. We were sitting together in the food court with a meal of dumplings and ramen.

"Nope," I said around a mouthful of noodles. Hope flared in my chest, warm and zinging. "You?"

Stef smiled and shook her head.

"I know it's a long ways away, but you should come visit my bookstore sometime." I couldn't believe those words popped out of my mouth.

"I would love that." Stef smiled and touched my hand. The zinging in my chest tingled all the way through my body.

Shivering, I tuck the memory away. No way is a gorgeous woman like Stef going to call someone like me.

Sighing and forcing the tears to the back of my eyes, I clap as my three friends cross the finish line Stef set up for them.

"Thank you, everyone for your hard work over the last few days!" Stef hollers, high-fiving everyone. But me. Everyone but me.

I swear, I'm not petty or jealous.

"You are now ready to begin your biking lives back home." Stef walks over to the cubbies by the door and pulls out three helmets in different sizes. They are brand new, the helmets we'd all trained in having been recycled. "These are for you. You earned them. Be safe and enjoy your new bikes!"

She hands one each to Georgie, Frank, and Henrietta as they leave, hugging each one. I pull my backpack on and slink over to the door. Bruises cover my body. I have nothing to show for it.

"We'll figure something out, Jordyn." Stef steps in and hugs me hard. My skin tingles, and my bruises ping with pain. "I promise, I won't let this be the end for you. We'll figure it out."

While I recover from her full body touching my full body, she pulls out my tablet, opens it, and puts her number in my contacts.

"I want to hear all about how your bookstore is doing," she says, handing me the tablet. "And I'd like to meet your dad someday. He sounds amazing."

"He is," I rasp out. "Thank you for trying, Stef."

I turn away before she can see the tears fall down my cheeks.

·   ·   ·

"Here we are." The cabbie jumps off their bike and pulls my suitcase out. I swipe my wrist and stand in front of my tiny house, smiling. It doesn't feel like a happy smile. But being home is nice.

"Jordyn!" Dad steps out of the front door, swiping away the thin branches of the weeping willow leaning over the front door. "I think I'm going to have to figure out how to buy another car," I say to Dad, leaning against him.

"I know, Bean." Dad strokes my back and hair. "Let's talk about it over dinner. I'll help if I can."

A week passes. Then another. I message and talk with Georgie. They became the closest of my three bike-class friends. I also chat with Henrietta, Frank waving from the background. I haven't heard from Stef at all. I try not to think about her. Or let the hurt in. I focus on work, and Dad, and Rosco. The last of whom is hell-bent on making me pay for leaving him for five days.

I call my bike cabbie for the night and am stepping out of the bookshop's back door to lock up when a tinkling bell sounds behind me. I turn.

Stef.

Stef is behind me. With something that looks sort of like a three-wheeled bike.

"Stef?" My brain can't catch up with my racing heart. "Stef?"

"Hi, Jordyn." Stef smiles at me. "How are you?"

"I—" I have to stop. "Stef?"

She starts laughing and jogs the few steps to me to grab my hand. I follow mutely.

"This is for you," she says, sweeping her hands out to the bike-thing. I stand, mouth agape.

The bike-thing is beautiful. It has three wheels, two up front, one in the back. It gleams in the lowering sunlight, shining happily at me.

"You found me a tricycle," I blurt out. "This is a fucking tricycle."

"I told you we'd figure it out." Stef gently bumps my shoulder with hers. I stumble a little and she catches me. "And technically, I made it for you. Get on and let's see how you like it."

"I love it," I say, turning to grin at her. Stef made me a tricycle? Stef made me a tricycle!

She pulls a helmet out of the bag by the trike and hands it to me.

"Congratulations, you passed your tricycle lessons."

Jamming the helmet on my head, I swing a leg over the trike. It's perfect. I pedal around the old parking lot behind the bookshop. I don't fall. The trike doesn't wobble under me. I will definitely have to build up more muscle to handle the hills. But that is a future worry.

I jump off the trike and grab Stef in a hug.

"I told you we'd figure it out," she whispers again in my ear. "Anyone who loves Melissa Chambers as much as I do is worth making a trike for."

Laughing, I lean into her.

EVERY WORD COUNTS

Elly Blue

Every word counts. Make sure

Make ev

The ballpoint pen faded to a whisper. I placed it reverently on the notepad, offering a small prayer of thanks for its service in bridging the old world and the new. The light from the afternoon sun briefly flared on the embossed words "Rick's Autobody—Milwaukie, Oregon," as if in acknowledgement. The notepad, above the looping cursive I'd cultivated since third grade, bore the Viagra logo, which had been hilarious when we found the pallet of them, but now just served as another daily reminder of our countless small losses.

A vivid sensory image flashed into my mind: sitting at my first computer, a boxy Dell, cross-legged in a rocking chair in my first apartment, the feeling of the keyboard, its soft clicking as I typed, the words flowing freely in that first fantasy novel, the one I'd discarded, fending off the confusion of my first queer crush with loving descriptions of elves' inner lives as they worked together across political factions to save their village from a landslide.

I ran a finger over the words on the pen, the weight of the world that we lost thick in my throat. "Sentimental sweetheart," Liz would say, kissing my forehead, if she were home to see me this way. I took a deep breath, calmed by the image. I'd take a secure relationship over word processing software and ballpoint pens any day. Over any of it.

Even five years since the power went out for what proved to be the last time, I was still stopped in my tracks every day by the completeness of that transformation, embodied in some sign or memory of the swollen excesses of the world that Liz and I grew to adulthood in. Ballpoint pens, which I'd always treated as endlessly available, endlessly renewable, much to Liz's amused annoyance.

I ran my eyes, as I often did, along the carefully curated shelf just above my desk. Starting with my first book, a ridiculously optimistic fantasy novel called *Goblin Supermarket*, continuing with increasingly professional-looking books that I'd written and Liz and I had published with our company Cozy Futures. My name on the spine was soon interspersed with those of other authors, all so dear and lost to us now. Three quarters of the way down the shelf, my throat caught, as it always did, at the abrupt transition from fictional stories of people bringing out the best in each other to rough, stapled pamphlets full of terse, practical skills for doing the same thing in real life: How to tear down fences and grow enough food to survive. How to step on a nail and live to tell. The most recent, on community water stewardship and sanitation, had a proper glued binding, wrinkled but holding strong.

I brushed away tears and stood up, slowly because of the vertigo. At moments like this, the best way to stave off sadness was to go visit the pigs. Speaking of troublingly short lives and complicated gratitude. I took the covered dish of veggie scraps from the kitchen and walked slowly out to the pen, gently closing the screen door behind me.

Outside, though, my senses were jumbled: movement, noise, all out of place. It took a minute to recalibrate my expectations, for my brain to adjust to the new story unfolding. The pigs were not in their pen; the gate hung open on one hinge. They were, however, in the vegetable garden, rooting around with merry desperation like they were clearing out the chest freezer at an apoc party.

With mild resignation, they let me lead them back through their gate, which I secured for now with bits of twisted wire, looped between the two battered old bike frames that Liz had built the gate out of: her old steel road bike, and my electric assist. With a sigh, I handed them the veggie scraps from the kitchen even though they'd just had a fresh feast. "Gather ye rosebuds while you may," I told them. Was that even the quote? No easy way to go look it up now.

This activity had exhausted me, so I sat down right in the middle of the vegetable bed and surveyed the damage.

The pigs had trampled and rooted up more than they'd eaten. I patted some potatoes back into the ground, retied a tomato plant, contemplated a large zucchini with a chunk taken out of it by a hoof. Not unrecoverable damage, but we might need to borrow more than we gave for the next few weeks. And we'd be bringing squash to the neighborhood dinner.

I heard a familiar soft crunch. Liz glided down the driveway path, half dismounted, standing on one pedal. "Not the pigs again?" she said, hopping off and leaning her bike against the shed. The cargo bed at the front of the bike was laden with twine-tied parcels—those must be the seed-saving zines, I thought.

"Yeah, I was hoping you could do a little better of a job than I did with the gate." I gesture to the wire. "They're getting crowded in the pen." I swallowed and kept patting the mound of dirt around the potatoes even though it didn't need it.

"I'll talk to Bella tomorrow. You're running low on thyroid stuff anyhow."

We sat contemplating the pigs, who were napping off the excitement of their wild rumpus, unaware that they'd been raised for butchery by a couple of lifelong vegans. The pigs—their thyroids, to be specific—are the reason I'm alive, albeit slower, colder, and more brittle than before. Their lives for mine. I never forget it for an instant.

Liz put a comforting hand on my shoulder. Then withdrew it, and I felt her tension. "What's wrong?"

"I should have been here," she said.

"Why? You wouldn't have stopped them getting out."

"But I could keep their pen better maintained. And it's not just this. There was the antpocalypse. And the leak in our bedroom. There's so much deferred maintenance around here that I can't get to when I'm gone all day. And the neighbors have done so much for us, it's time I started helping them at least a fraction of that."

"So teach Amal, she's got a handy streak. And now that she's done with school, she could do more around the house and neighborhood." In fact, my niece had been planning to move in with her date two neighborhoods over, but bringing that up would do nothing to strengthen my argument.

"Listen," said Liz. "Really, listen. I would have been here four hours ago, that was my plan. But my front tire finally blew out, up by the press."

It was my turn to put a comforting hand on her back. As with ballpoint pens, we were nearing the end of the shelf life of manufactured rubber products, and it was amazing how much everything Liz did revolved around finding replacements for those. Bikes and printing presses both require rubber, lubricant, solvents, fiddly mechanical parts. We'd been stockpiling resources, and it turns out there's a lot you can find a workaround for, but even those dwindling supplies were dissolving, rotting, changing into something less useful but no less toxic.

"Looks like you got it sorted," I gesture to her cargo bike, with its two functional tires.

"Yeah, but I had to go halfway to Troutdale, slow as fuck on a dollar boot. The guy had a bunch of sixteen-inchers in decent shape, but he was handsy." A shiver went through her body. "I made a real impression on him, he won't mess with the next person. But seriously, Julie, this is all to say—I think this is a sign."

No! I wanted to exclaim, but I held back, seeing the tears in Liz's eyes. She looked away and so did I, at the shambles of the garden; at the snorfling, satisfied pigs; at the neighbor kid skipping out of a back door across the block and pulling down water from a barrel; at the shade trees that had witnessed a lifetime of human upheaval and would outlive us to witness far more.

"You've been planning your retirement in secret, haven't you?" I said, and she looked at me in surprise, then grinned and let out her dear bark of a laugh.

"You know me too well. Let's just say I've been hedging my bets. A plan to stay and a plan to go. Do you want to go inside?"

I stretched out a hand. Liz levered herself up with enviable ease and reached down to pull me up, too.

"It's not the press," she said, matching my hobble over to the back steps, hopping ahead to hold the screen door open for me. "I could do that every day for my entire life. Making sure people have books to keep them going. Did I tell you about the submission we got this week, instructions for homemade sex toys and lube? That's a vital service right there. Plus, you know Chris won't be as careful about paper thickness without me breathing down their neck. And I wasn't going to quit before I solved the westside distribution problem. And after that, there's north of the river. . . ."

"But you can't get to the press without the bike, and keeping the bike running is taking up all your time that you could be using to ferry smutty zines to Vancouver by raft." She stuck out her tongue at me as I collapsed onto the couch in a small puff of dust, sending up a tiny prayer of mourning for vacuum cleaners. "I get it," I said with a sigh. "You love your bicycle, but it's the weak link."

"Yeah!" she said, already fiddling with the handle on the cistern tap. Then she looked at me more sharply. "Wait a minute, Jules, stop with that."

"Stop with what? You have a weakness for a weak link. It's endearing. And I'm personally thankful."

"Sometimes," she said, "the squeaky wheel gets the grease because it needs and deserves grease, and because it happens to be very close friends with the manager of a grease factory, and then it ends up being the wheel that keeps everyone else turning even when things seem pretty fucking hopeless."

"Not to get carried away with a completely different metaphor."

"Spending four years in the wild world of postapocalyptic nonfiction publishing has made me respect metaphors a little less. Do you really still see yourself as a liability?"

"I mean, not in the same way as your bike is one." I said it with a teasing tone, but she was all seriousness now, perching next to me on the arm of the couch in that spring-loaded, energetic way of hers and handing me a glass of water.

"It doesn't have to mean giving anything up," she said, fierce. "You know, in the before times, I wasn't going to be able to retire. I was going to die at my desk. I convinced myself it was because I loved what we were doing with Cozy Futures. And I did. I loved publishing your books and I loved doing it with you. And it's been incredible to get to rebuild the way we have. But you know what? Sitting by the fire with you, tending the garden, keeping the pigs happy and the house standing, being a functional part of the neighborhood, raising Amal's kids? That sounds like about five full-time jobs I'd love to have, and I would take any or all of them over chasing around town, without you, fighting this uphill battle against material obsolescence. And soon, I'll start falling apart at this rate, too. I don't want to wait for one more broken bone." She touched her collarbone with a grimace. That break had taken her off her feet for two restless months that neither of us enjoyed much, and it still caused her pain a year later.

"I've still got plenty of ideas for books," she continued. "Bean and Mike are more than ready to take over the day-to-day. And it'd be easier to keep the bike in usable condition if I'm not riding it into the ground every day. Same with my knees. I could still bring our manuscripts up there, grab some distribution on my way home. It wouldn't be the end of the world." We both smiled at that, our old gallows joke as the world we knew had fallen apart around us.

"I guess it's time to show you what I've been workin on," I told her.

"The thing about pig keeping?"

"Too depressing, I've been procrastinating with something else. Grab the notepad from my desk. I wasn't going to show you yet, but it seems timely."

She leapt up and scooped up my draft, 25 scrawled pages advertising Viagra and carefully describing the process of publishing a book in the now times. "I'll need you to add the technical bits," I said. "But if you need to stop, if you need to have a final project, it should be this one. So what you've created can be carried on."

The expression on Liz's face as she stood in the last low rays of sun, leafing through the pages, was a treasure I stored in my memory to keep with me for the rest of my life.

"We'll need a section for different types of presses, and hand-printing techniques," she said. "And we could get Berry to do a chapter on paper and ink." She put the pages back on the desk and came to sit facing me on the couch, cross-legged, grinning. "I see I wasn't the only one planning my retirement in secret. Very clever. But you're aware this may backfire? It's going to inspire competition, and you know how much I love a challenge."

I whacked her gently with a pillow. "It'll inspire collaboration, partnerships. It's only oldies like us who still think like everything's an individual effort."

"Except you, you were ahead of the rest of us in that regard. That's why everyone loved your books so much. Julie, do you ever miss writing fiction? You were so talented at it, and you gave it up so completely."

I take a breath, feeling the exhaustion, also the contentment of my body, our home, our conversation, the world around us. "I sometimes think I should miss it, but I don't. You know, I think I wrote it to try to slow life down a little. It always felt like the world was getting away from me, I wanted to make sense of it and to create these stories that could help people find a way to feel better. But now, every day is like a year used to be, and what's important is so crystal clear every second of every day."

Liz leaned in for a kiss, and time slowed down even more.

We both went back outside, me to the composting toilet and Liz to fix and strengthen the gate. "Thank you," I mouthed to the pigs on my way back in.

Writing the story of my life is something I would never do in the now times, not with our dwindling resources. But if I were to write it, I'd discard all rules about plot and narrative arc. I'd neglect the crises and big dramatic events and just capture the sweetest moments when I felt the real-world version of the magic that I used to try to capture in fantasy novels.

I sat at my desk, pulled a fresh pen out of the drawer, and continued where I'd left off. *Make every word count.*

OF BOUNTIES AND BOOKS

Kathryn Reilly

Parking her bike on the icy expanse, Ella dismounts, running her hands lovingly over Bennet's curves. The modified saddlebags hang empty, but hopefully she'll struggle to close the clasps soon. *Bennet's a beast and will certainly ensure we'll make it back to the ship in one piece*, Ella thinks, *this run is like any other, just a bit deeper*. Some might argue it's silly to name a bike, but she knows it's all about the energy. Kitted out with a deep, studded tread, Bennet glides through the snowy landscape as if navigating the yellow brick road without a worry in the world.

Pressing a button on her bike's handlebars, she deactivates the antigravity feature; Bennet hovers sleek as a hummingbird over long distances, but Ella always rides her for the sheer fun of it closer to their destination. Arriving at the destination, a second button anchors four long spikes into the ice, creating bedrock-strong stability for what Ella has to do next: tunnel through the icy tundra, then lower herself, inch by inch, seeking the bounties. A third button activates Bennet's internal warming system to keep the planet's bone-numbing cold at bay. Dangerously low temperatures could turn her tires brittle, and hauling herself and her cargo would be problematic, so she'd designed a simple system to keep them both safe.

Hefting the modified tunneling device onto her shoulder, Ella extends the tripod supports, securing them to the bike using specialized clamps she'd welded herself. Pressing the communicator, she speaks clearly, watching the coordinates scroll within her helmet's screen. "Arya, I'm here, Bennet's stable, and I'd like to double-check the coordinates."

"Of course, Captain. Coordinates should read 39.9476 degrees north and 75.1358 degrees west. Weather conditions in this region are good for the next 48 hours. Target's depth is approximately sixty feet, so you'll need to evaporate the ice melt as you go."

"Copy. Arya, thanks." Ella climbs onto her bike, standing on the seat, working to align the laser according to the GPS coordinates. Balancing, she activates the laser, hoping the ancient map the clients on planet T42n loaned her is accurate enough. Lucky for her, when these clients' ancestors evacuated Earth, their emergency bag contained a map marked with interesting attractions and hearts surrounding used bookstores. Useless in space, the paper denoting highways and roadside attractions in a place called Pennsylvania became a family heirloom, a peek into what Earth had been before becoming an endless white planet.

Obtaining use of the map had been a difficult trade; she'd guaranteed the family first choice for five books from her salvages, plus the return of their map within three years. After a centuries-old climate event, one could never expect things to remain where old Earth maps said they once resided, so Ella crosses her fingers that the bookstore survived beneath the ice.

Recovering humanity's best lost treasures always spiked her senses; her blood thrummed, adrenaline coursing, readying for discovery. Ella hoped to add a few new gems to her personal hoard. Nearly sixty feet down, the laser shuts off, and Ella peers into a darkness surely resembling the one Otto, Axel, and Hans navigated in their adventures towards the center of the Earth. Having checked all her gear, she tosses a rope into the depths and begins rappelling down, the ghosts of Verne's characters chattering in her head. "Well, let's hope this journey is without cave-ins, lava, or prehistoric terrors, but an underground ocean would be pretty cool," she muses aloud. Touching her communicator, she speaks to her ship, "Arya, I'm heading down now."

"Acknowledged, Captain. Would you like me to review the top priority books?"

"Yes, and their clues."

"Accessing. Here are top priorities. Remember, you cleared the transport room, so you can haul four hundred books this trip, give or take. With your bike you can haul sixty to seventy, so six or seven trips. We might be able to push storage to five hundred if the volumes are smaller, or if you discover many paperbacks in good condition. Six VIP bounties: (1) *The Count*—love and adventure story; prison; tricks rich people; happy ending, (2) *Watership*—lots and lots of rabbits; one of them dreams; bad, big rabbit, (3) *Giovanni and His House*—love tale; figuring life out, (4) *Butterflies*—about butterflies; starts on a farm in the mountains; author is a king, (5) *Shannara*—made up realm with magic; lots and lots of magic, and (6) *Frankenstein*—created life; monster; villain scientist; storms; female author? Finding *Frankenstein* would be particularly good as the client guaranteed fuel as well as fresh and canned produce."

"Received. Continue to monitor the transport room for optimal temperature. Continuing descent." Ella smiles, remembering how proud her parents had been when she'd designed and welded her ship. Not a huge one, mind, just one the right size for discovering the Verse. Besides the bridge, it offers comfy quarters, a tiny galley, a larger storage room for her bike and books, and a whatever room, for well, whatever she needed it to do: sometimes food storage, or client transport, or really however she could make a buck out here on her own. One arm's length of rope at a time, Ella lowers herself deeper into the darkness, ice smooth as glass 360 degrees around her.

On a frozen planet, or any planet really, there's no better way to pass the time than hunting books. Well, reading them, certainly—but she had to excavate them first. Humans flung themselves wide around the Verse; histories of The Event speak of animals and people frozen within moments, trapped still beneath the frozen tundras. Perhaps one day scientists would dissect their stomach contents and puzzle over what Earth humans used to eat; but until then, books she unearthed could describe the most wondrous meals: fast foods, and giant ostrich eggs, and turducken, and lava cakes, and something called sushi that seemed to be somewhat complicated. She and Arya often discussed the food in stories. Space may be loneliness personified, but if one waits it out, adventure lays herself bare before the brave. Ella skirted the loneliness with a clever ship AI who loved puns.

"Hey, Arya?"

"Yes, Captain?"

"How much farther down?"

"Perhaps twenty feet or so; your signal is weakening. Captain, if this run is a successful one, can we have a party after to celebrate?"

"Sure, Arya, we can have a party."

"Excellent, Captain, and don't worry, I'll planet!"

"Nice one, Arya. I see the structure below; this new headlamp was worth the trade. I'm going offline while I axe through the structure. Captain out."

This moment was always her favorite: the moment right before discovery. Worlds of words existed just beneath her feet. For months, she'd planet-hopped among human settlements, taking book requests and negotiating payments. She even charged a small fee for people to come aboard and listen to books she'd recorded before turning them over to clients or auctioning them off; she had to pass the time somehow traveling to and from Earth across the Verse. Her livelihood was chancy; sometimes bounties took years, but shepherding a book back to its human was always worth it. *Stories haunt us*, she thought, *reaching ever for resurrection.*

Like Sherlock, Ella kept a tablet recording clues clients remembered from the oral stories their great-grands shared. She noted characters, plots, images, illustrations, authors . . . but these recollections were often incorrect. After centuries of retellings, storytellers inserting and deleting as they wished to make the story their own, hunting these memories demanded a profession of patience. Nevertheless, she loved it; she loved descending the darkness, recapturing imaginations bound in paper, and releasing stories from their icy tombs.

Fully extending her legs to stand on the roof, a startling *clang* reverberated. Ella froze, unsure. She picked up her left boot with ice spikes and put it down on the roof again. *Clang.* She stomped: *clang. This is new*, she thought. Kneeling, she let out a breath. "It's metal. The roof is metal," her voice echoed up the tunnel. "Well, this will be a bit harder to hack through." She prepared herself before setting about using the axe to pry off the metal tiles. Placing them to the side, she resolved to take them with her. "I'm discovering new things all the time, just like Alice," she muttered before starting to hack a hole through the wooden supports until her muscles screamed mercy. Once, a client requested "*Wonderful*—girl falls down a hole chasing a rabbit." Not unlike what she was doing now, tunneling down, down, but hopefully without the falling part. Her client recalled maybe there was a queen, but there were definitely weird hats and a thing called a walrus. Another client knew the girl's name was Alice, and that golden clue made her story so much easier to find. Ella had never met a queen, but she did have to tunnel down quite a bit to find *Alice's Adventures in Wonderland*, somewhere in the state of Vegas. Safely nestled in a library forty feet down, she had found a beautifully bound copy portraying a young girl in a blue dress. Ella remembered being captivated by the dress; she'd never seen anything quite like it. Most beings across the Verse wore something similar to pants, because pockets; everyone needed spaces to keep all the things, and pants could be made with many pockets, and even secret pockets. Looking down, Ella counted nine pockets, and two small, secret ones sewn into the waist part of her pants. One never knew when a vial of Slofphinka poison might come in handy—it was always better to be prepared. She also had four loops and a place for the axe which she clipped back into its designated spot.

Wiggling to the hacked hole's edge, Ella's feet dangled above what looked like a checkout counter. Her headlamp illuminated shelves and shelves of books; giddy, she took a moment to ensure her heat and oxygen regulators were circulating well. Bowing her head, she softly spoke a prayer, "Stories recall our histories and our hopes, allowing ourselves to reinvent the world again and again and again. May the stories be found and shared forever." Picking up the rope, Ella dropped the last ten feet inside.

Disconnecting, she stepped into history and imagination. It thrummed with possibility, offering Ella a favorite smell: old, musty paper and ink. The building hadn't hosted humans in centuries, yet their presence remained. Surely ancient humans treated book houses as holy. A bit ago, she'd stumbled upon a highly desired story. The client had given Ella "*Martian Stories—stories about going to space, author Ray.*" And Ella came across it tunneling into a library somewhere on the land of Australia.

Walking past a nonfiction section, Ella remembered *The Martian Chronicles* as a good book; it rooted into her brain long after she'd finished reading its stories. It made her think of her great-great-great-great-great-grandparents' diary, recording their migration, much like the characters in these stories. The absolute silence surrounding her unsettled Ella just a bit, so she activated her story archive. "Play Grand's diary, entry four."

"Rocket sky is what we remember, thousands of rockets fleeing, and though we couldn't see, we knew those watching us were corpses, just not quite yet. Our employer says Millarium will be our refuge. Its turquoise soils are inhospitable to the few seeds we smuggled aboard, and we leave a bit more of ourselves and knowledge behind every day to survive in this new world. Greg says we'll be fine, but I wonder if our fate and the fate of our children is to become aliens. We have no home but for the one we will carve out, one that another planet will allow us. And we will become that place, ever-adapting."

"Play Grand's diary, entry twenty-eight."

"Greg and I weld most of the day, but, in the evenings, I am learning the flowers of this world, which hum. If you sit with them, humming in return, they'll gift you a nectar, used to sweeten foods and drinks. But unlike Earth, the flowers thrive in the three moons' light, and I must hum in the softened darkness."

Ella thought *The Martian Chronicles* captured the hope and hardship humanity's lineage felt for sure. All captains feel that awe, and the fear, looking at the stars, she knew from experience. But they continue to leave, exploring while yearning for homes they can only ever now know in stories. Stepping into this building, shelves lined with books, Ella feels as though she stands within the house that continued on in the story without the people. In silence, the building remembers people; the carpet reveals their favorite paths; worn spines hint towards favorite stories; knickknacks speak to a love of cats. Terrariums share their love of plants, dust though they may be.

Following the arrows for fiction to the back of the shop, Ella stops short. There, in a chair, sat a bespeckled man, frozen. He could have been sleeping, save for the blue tinge settled across his sunken skin. His eyes were closed, and a mound of blankets lay at his feet, knee-high with a folded note on top, For You scrawled in elegant, faded script.

Carefully, Ella unfolds the note:

These are my most favorite books. I've covered them as best I can. I stayed and read them as long as my fingers could turn the pages. Humanitys oldest known book is over 1,200 years old, I hope that it doesnt take quite so long to discover these treasures. Love them as so many of us did.

Thomas

Carefully, she removes the blankets to find stacked books, forty-one in total. Opening her pack, she transfers them, noting that *Frankenstein* and *The Count of Monte Cristo* are among the books Thomas thought worth saving. Tucking his note into her suit, she turns and walks among the aisles, seeking the best preserved fiction titles.

Getting her bearings, Valentine Michael Smith pops into her mind, and she remembers hunting for his story. "*Stranger Land*—human born in space comes to Earth, thinks humans are weird." Like him, she is a human born on an alien world returning to find her ancestral home curious and vexing; *Earth is the alien planet to us all now*, Ella thinks. During a bounty hunt, she loves peeking into drawers and cupboards, discovering items used once upon a time; every now and again, she pockets something interesting, loving the mystery of puzzling out its purpose.

Taking off her pack, she examines shelved books, hoping time hasn't ravaged the paper too much. Several shelves later, *Watership Down* appears. Bingo! Gorgeous illustrations of furred creatures with tall ears peer at Ella from the pages. *These must be the rabbits*, she thinks. She's never seen anything quite like them. Her fingers trace over embossed leather, faded but protecting the story inside. Inside the front cover is a map; *all the best stories come with maps*, she smiles.

Pack full, she winds her way back to her rope, pausing to thank the bookkeeper before attaching steel ice spikes on her shoes. "Ready, Bennet," and she presses a button; she can't hear the slow whirl, but the rope grows taunt, and she holds tight as the steel spikes find purchase in the ice as Bennet pulls her up. During the slow, steady ascent, she recalls *"Earthseas—magic and adventures, Wizard Ged, evil shadow,"* and wonders how many of the stories she'd just collected will share more magical realms. Humanity survives among Le Guin's imagined worlds now, whose inhabitants' technologies sometimes make magic look real. *We remember our mythic monsters and heroes most of all: kraken, werewolves, La Llorona, Carmilla, and Odysseus, Katniss, Beowulf, Hermione, Arwen, Janie*, she considers. These stories are always in high demand because mostly, humans triumph and need the reminder that dragons can be slayed. For while dragons weren't real on Earth, far worse monsters stalk the Verse. The flargoyums on Millarium spit acid, boring holes through flesh and bone instantly; her great-great-great-great-grandmother lost an arm to a territorial flargoyum. *There's no one better to have in your corner than your ancestors whispering through words that dragons can (almost) always be slain*, she thinks.

Bennet stops pulling, and Ella digs the spikes as deep as she can to leverage herself and her bounties over the icy edge. Crawling towards her bike, she finally stands and begins transferring the books into the waiting saddlebags. Full, she presses the communicator button, "Arya?"

"Good to hear your voice, Captain."

"It was a successful run. We'll be able to stock the ship just from this bookstore, with a few knickknacks as well. And! There are a few landscape calendars—those always sell well."

"Do the landscape images have lots of trees?"

"Of course. Why?"

"Captain, do you know the difference between weather and climate?"

"Please tell me Arya."

"Well, you can't weather a tree, but you can climate!"

"That might be your best pun in a while, Arya. I'm heading back to unload and refuel Bennet and myself. I should be able to complete two more runs today. Let's plan on staying three days if the weather holds."

"Noted, Captain. See you soon."

Ella removes her ice spikes, curls the rope, and nestles both into the backpack with the metal tiles. She disassembles the laser and stows it as well. Then, swinging a leg over Bennet, she presses the button to retract the stabilizing spikes. "Ship coordinates," she speaks aloud, and a map pops up before her eyes. Then she's off, speeding towards her ship, tires crunching the top layers of ice, the icy planet's air whooshing by her.

Ella thinks about the stories she'll find homes for, about how the moment she places a bounty in the hands of its new owner, light radiates from their eyes. Hope and history and home explode, mingling, as their fingers caress the binding and their eyes, eager, devour the words that rekindle realms lost to them. *Nearly everyone left books behind since their pages couldn't feed people or ships; in the chaos, no one remembered they fed souls. And as refugees, we crave them, Ella thinks, centuries later, we still crave the the quieter stories of perseverance and self-discovery, but we need adventure and fantasy stories most of all—the stories spinning great odds, daunting unknowns, unimaginable realities, and survival in the end. We most needed our best myths when we left them behind.*

They're coming, Ella thinks, speeding on Bennet across a moon-white world. *I'm bringing our stories home.*

WE BECOME WHO WE ARE

Kiera Jessica Bane

I fell asleep that night thinking of bicycles. When I awoke, I found myself free . . .

*T*wake up, stand, stretch, and get dressed. It's a story any woman over the age of 25 knows: your spine just isn't what it used to be. There's a tightness and slouching to my posture I'm now aware I have to keep in check. And that's just part of growing up, or at least growing old. I hook my sports bra, spin it 180, shoulders through the arms, dump my silicone tits into the cups, and inhale sharply as I zip the front closure into remarkable, but tight, cleavage. The rest of my attire is summer simple: shorts and, as my girlfriend tells me, an inappropriately short crop top. The heat outside turns the air of the bedroom muggy and uncomfortable. I check myself in the mirror, and as I turn side-on to see which parts curve and which parts bulge, the reflection of sunlight glares from my forehead, into the mirror, and back into my eyes.

My head often aches from the titanium housing of my implants. I know as well as my silent clinicians do that the optical processor is compacting my spinal column. It's tolerable once I'm warm. I loosen up in the heat and motion, the warm breeze melting my body into wholeness. I'm happy with how my implant looks, despite it being a sheet of polished metal covering my scalp from temple to just behind my ear. The cyborgs of science fiction have always been my favorite characters anyway. Now I relate in a literally augmented way.

The implant helps me process the world. If you don't have a sensory processing disorder, you can never quite understand the onslaught that hypersensitivity makes the commonplace. I used to find direct light, especially the sunlight, to be unbearable. With the internal dimmers of my implant, I can reduce the light exposure. It's like wearing transition lenses. I can finally separate sounds and assimilate the information comfortably with the data buffers without the need for a blanket and a dark, silent room.

The sweat.
The chafing of the silicon.
The ribs rubbed raw.

I rinse and fill my bottle with water cold enough that condensation forms on the exterior of the vessel; with each use, the stickers adorning it warp and bleed their color, aging like the trusted tools they are. I do pre-ride checks on my bicycle for all the basics: tire pressure, puncture repair kit, small tools, and a pump. I throw in a few snacks and a book, and strap a picnic blanket to the pannier rack, hoping to find somewhere to stop and sit for a while, read, or, fickle woman that I am, otherwise bake in the heat. I'm allergic to grass, and there's nothing else where I'm heading.

Helmet on, music up, focused: I leave the city.

It's easier than ever to ride these days. In fact, a lot of people, the ones still here, who were warned against using cars, motorbikes, and other motorized vehicles, have taken to cycling. You can always tell the newbies: no helmet or masks on them. They're not seasoned enough to know what a near miss with a bus makes you thankful for. With nearly one-third of my head coated in a metal plate, it can be tempting to ride without a helmet, but a pileup is still a pileup, whether it's started by automobiles or bicycles. If you thought roadside repairs were tricky on your flashy carbon frame, try to imagine the repair on your semi-metal skull.

Even with more cyclists hitting the road, I'm not crowded. I can outpace all but the hardcore in their Lycra skin suits. I'm happy to not be one of them.

I don't wear headphones on my leisure cycles. A speaker sits in my bar bag and blasts music straight up into my face. With the background roar of the city subdued by the diminished population, I don't need the volume high at all. I've learned to appreciate all types of music when cycling. Certain grooves fit the pedals like a cleat: jazz for the uphill climbs, funk or pop for the flats, and for the exhilarating downhills, I like grindcore.

The places I like to go are rarely ever popular; the trade-off being poorly maintained roads littered with potholes and crumbling away at the edges. At least there is no fear of mangling death now that cars are a rare luxury. I seldom know where I'm going when I leave. Just the cliché of an open road, breeze in my hair. On the straights, I'm sometimes bold enough to lift my top up, bare my chest to the wind, and try to cool off my sweatier crevices.

I know the risk I'm taking when I do this. A woman far from a built-up area, and a cybernetic one at that, knows the danger of being alone in unfamiliar surroundings. I see things coming faster than other people, oftentimes before they even happen. Before the implant, I saw every detail of my surroundings ahead of me as a scrambled mess of rigid color. I still see everything the same, but now it's like I can slow the world around me for a few moments to allow my brain to catch up. For safety's sake, I still carry a set of barbed knuckles when I ride. I don't go out to stay safe. I go out to be brave, to prove it can be done. I suppose the end isn't so bad, after all, if you can keep two wheels ahead of it.

The constant of rearranging.
The excruciating, unforgiving saddle.
The unpredictable road threatening to throw my identity into the sunlight.

It all seemed to start as a joke. It was happening "over there" instead of here, and the distance gave almost everyone on the planet a sense of safety. I was no different: I had little idea of what was happening until it hit. And by then, it was already too late for hundreds of thousands of people. It gave the feeling that we were being wiped out. As if the pavements wouldn't be filled with the same throngs of people that had occupied them before. I didn't want anyone to die, but I was equally happy to have breathing room from the chaos. Some tasteless quip that humans are the disease, as if millions of years of evolution had specific prophetic wisdom just for them. The conspirators are always the first to jump the shark: "It was planned!" "It happens every hundred years!", etc. . . . Of course, what they all failed to grasp were two things: the simple collusive properties of capitalism, and the obliteration of the natural world. Something about knowing my pedal power staves off industrial growth feels liberating—like I'm not making an acid rain cloud for the kids to grow up under. The kids are sweet, but I ride alone.

I ride until I think I'm there. A feeling inside me tells me when to stop. When to squeeze the brakes and find a spot to sit for a while. If I can hear only the wind and the birds, perhaps the rustle of a startled deer bounding out of its overgrown resting place, it is a good place to stop. I find somewhere suitable to park myself. I opt to leave my bicycle in the shade of a tree to keep the heat from my perishables, but I prefer to feel the sun on my thighs as I recline. I'm pale all year round, regardless of what I do, besides my forearms. The hair on my forearms is less present as it turns golden with my tanning arms.

I take a few hungry but steady gulps of water. I drink as if I'm a castaway, assuring myself of enough fluid for my respite and the return cycle. The heat kills you if you're not careful. I lay out the blanket and pull out my book. I love the antiquated feel of a printed book but my e-reader gives me weightless options. I store more than I think I could ever read. Titles on prison abolition, long-standing refutes of land ownership, and less provocative reads on space and robots fill the digital space that I float on. Angela Davis usually wins, but today I want to become astral. I want to coast on the weightless words that lift the mind from the Earth. I want to believe in a place that doesn't suppress the individual. My taste in nonfiction usually leads me to ludicrous titles like *Android Avenger*, *March of the Robots*, or, the particularly absurd *Zarkon, Lord of the Unknown*. Fun as these titles are, the books themselves scarcely touch the possibilities of the human condition or distract from my reality as do those by Frederik Pohl. His words build worlds in my imagination.

Laying on my side upon a grassy incline, I take stock of my body: what hurts and what shouldn't. I usually try in vain for a tan on my thighs and upper arms, but my breasts and back make it stressful to lay on my front for very long while I read. I feel the sweat over my chest and decide that I have enough privacy to make a few wardrobe changes. My trainers and socks are the first to come off as I adore the fresh feeling of the blanket against my soles, followed by my top. The sports bra underneath covered more than the top did anyway. If I were truly fearless, I'd unhook it and let the breeze caress me. It takes more strength than I have to let myself live in that natural state. I know how unlikely it is that I might be seen here. Perhaps the eyes I'm most afraid of seeing my body are my own. I'm constantly embarrassed by the fact that my boobs fall out. Not in a "nip-slip" fashion but in a "crash to the ground" way. Though realistic, they are heavy, and the seams betray their synthetic origin. Ironic that I should be so ashamed of this hidden prosthesis and not the obvious metal adorning my head. I'm not brave enough to lose them, not brazen enough to confront years of internalized sexism and to think of myself as a woman without breasts. To defend myself by demanding my pronouns be used. It should be so easy. But I'm not brave enough.

Tank top exposing hidden hair.
Cycle shorts do the same.
The sweat always irritates the places I wish to change.

It should be so easy. It was simple enough to get a chunk of metal and wires implanted into my skull, how hard can it be to have boobs? When it was first proposed that humans could be given technological enhancements, it was inevitably parried by bioessentialist reactionaries asking if they should. Here, in my spit of the former empire, there was little debate around cybernetic implants. It was widely regarded as no different to giving an amputee a replacement limb. Although there were a few small sects of the overly indoorsy and religious to question just how far the cybernetic process could go, their concerns were swiftly silenced by the decimation of the planet. I didn't see the irony at the time, but it occurs to me now that I waited six months in total for my cerebral implants, including the consultation period. I'd already been waiting longer than that for gender-affirming hormones. I'm still waiting now.

My breasts are fillers. Flesh-colored, wobbly silicone shaped like teardrops. The kind used by drag acts and mastectomy patients. They give me the shape I desire, but they itch, sweat, and rub the skin from my chest. I want more than anything to give my body the shape I need, the shape that will help me survive, but the world has its own agenda.

It was difficult enough before the bacteria swept across most of the known world, before medicine was pushed to the brink of collapse. In the first throes of the disease, the governments of the world turned on their own marginalized peoples in an onslaught of discrimination. Laws passed, policy created, hatreds affirmed. It felt like everyone knew it was happening, and they all. Just. Watched. It was never about bathroom safety or athleticism. It was never about security or justice. It was only ever about suppression and control. It was erasure, at a time when humans dropped like flies by the hundreds of thousands. And still they tried to kill us.

In the written word, these threats disappear. I can't be destroyed in pages, even when the Martians arrive. Societies I dream of become real, without poverty, without tyranny. I take confidence from the imaginary friends in text, glean the guidance I lack. The positronic wondering for a human existence. To become the flesh of identity. They change what they cannot accept. They become who they are, embracing the faults and overcoming the obstacles set by a predetermined physiology. And, I, through abstraction, share in their discomfort. Through the fictional eyes of machines, I learned authenticity of self.

My unwanted hair will be destroyed by lasers. My shape will evolve with the introduction of chemicals. My overloaded synapses calmed by artificial implants. The stuff of science fiction in the present day.

And to not live in the present day is foolish.

I sit up. I'm as isolated as the rest of the world. With no one here to see me but myself, I take a last look at my synthetic cleavage. I unzip my bra and allow my imitation tits to peel away from my body, an unceremonious departure, the protective shell giving way to vulnerability. My chest rejoices at this sudden unexpected ventilation and rises with my spirits as if to tell me I have made the right choice. For now, I tuck these away and roll onto my front to continue my sunkissed reading.

Slowly, my spine becomes looser. I am more comfortable inside and out. We become who we are, to live unrepentant as oneself in a universe so vast. How could there not be a place for me?

I think about a friend, distant and gone but ever present in their words. "You deserve to be here," she told me. It was a throwaway remark whilst I scoffed at my proximity to high-end petrol guzzlers, these appendages the upper middle classes couldn't be seen without. She squeezed my hand and spoke the words I didn't know I was looking for. She had torn down the barriers to my own self-acceptance and she didn't even know it. Those profound words have echoed in my mind ever since I last saw her, as a reminder of myself, a reminder that there is a place for me outside of everything I currently occupy. If the wheels or books should ever fail me, she would be there.

The bicycle wheels transcended the wheels of time, becoming the wheels of chance. The possibility of a future peace against the hate. The words couldn't be taken away. They are my adventure within the adventure. The portal to another place impossible dimensions away. When I ride, these things are obscured, hidden in the passing flash of traffic. When I ride, I focus only on what's ahead. When I ride, I'm free.

I cycle home, no longer fearful of potholes or the intrusive eyes of strangers, flat-chested and smiling. I drip with the success of my ride as I return. I run a bath and watch myself undress. I shine, not just a shimmer and not from the glistening sweat; I radiate in my own beauty. I won't suffer destroying myself for a body I do not yet have. I will own and love what I am now. We become who we are.

THE ENLIGHTENMENT OF DANA FINE

Aaron M. Wilson

Waking up in the morning holds two truths.

One, waking up signals that a new cycle has begun. The body has completed its period of required rest during which the subconscious mind processes the events from the previous cycle and the metabolic system flushes toxins. There is some other junk that happens, too, but those are the biggies.

Two, waking up signals a choice, and I'm going to Mr. Rogers this shit.

From Phoebe's lithium mining colony, the rings of Saturn are dim. All those pictures on the enlistment brochures are a lie. The rings show only a hint of color—not the promised "walking on rainbows." Lithium mines are the new strawberry fields. Promises of good pay, a better life. The fine print is that, upon arrival, you owe transport costs, uniform costs, food costs, water and even air costs. The pay doesn't cover the costs.

"You awake?"

I roll over. Sarah is buckling her standard-issue mining boots, white with blue seams and cheap plastic rollerblade-style compression buckles. "Hey, neighbor." I push up on one elbow.

"Breakfast in ten." She zips up her matching jacket and presses the green button at the center of her chest near the company logo, a blue blob striped with black. The logo is supposed to be ore but looks more like a rotten blueberry. The suit hums to life. The blue seams glow.

"Oh, yeah. I love me some juice," I say. Sarah picks up the 250-pound pickaxe that was leaning against the wall like it was an aluminum baseball bat.

"You don't want to miss breakfast again." She shakes her head and walks out the door. The door silently slides shut, no cool space-show sounds, just a click when it locks.

I hate breakfast—goo in a squeeze bottle. Today, however, I'm going to try to make friends. I pull out a thin paper book from under my pillow. A children's book. The happy man in a red sweater makes my eyes roll. "A beautiful day for a neighbor. . . ." it goes.

The hallways are five workers wide and about five and half feet high. Some of the taller miners have to stoop. There are arrows on the walls. Some have the company logo along them, showing the way to the mines. Others have red crosses for medical, green plants for gardening, and food for the mess hall.

The mess hall is enormous. It could seat five thousand, but there are three hundred and fifty of us. I know two other people here: Sarah and Mr. Dunken. Today, that changes.

Mr. Dunken is greeting miners as they enter, inspecting suits for charge, cleanliness, and defect.

I get my breakfast tube from the vending machine. It reads my account code and adds to my debt. I walk through the tables to one filled with large men laughing. It seems like a fun place to start. I plunk down at the table. "Hey, neighbors."

The conversation stops. They look at me, eyes wide.

The man with the mustache from another time laughs and bangs the table. His smile makes his mustache part and tremble. He holds out his hand, "Wats."

"Dana."

"Pleasure's all mine."

The table shifts as Wats stands to sit down next to me. I keep smiling.

"Don't mind this lot." He sweeps his arm wide. "We don't usually commiserate with new blood. It makes for sad feelings when they die in the tunnels." He swats me on the back.

"I've been here nine cycles." I put the breakfast tube in my pocket, suddenly not hungry. Why am I trying? This is stupid.

Wats grins. "I see you've been here long enough to save your food. Good girl." He finishes his tube and puts it down the hole in the center of the table. "We usually wait forty before getting friendly." His eyes twinkle. "You, though, I think you'll be fine," he lies, twitching his mustache.

"I don't see axes." I look around the table. "What do you do?"

"Nope. We're pedalers." He holds his arms out like he's gripping handlebars. "The trains don't move themselves, do they?" He laughs.

"How does one get to be a pedaler? That sounds better than swinging this." I hoist the axe into my lap.

"It is, but *you* don't." His face caves in on itself. He looks down the length of the table. "Time to saddle up, *men.*"

They get up, grumbling. Soon, everyone is standing and making their way out of the mess hall. I make my way to "train" C. It is a series of mining buckets on oversized wagon wheels connected to an "engine" at either end. I can't believe I missed that the engines were large four-wheeled bikes.

I spot Wats at the front of train E. His mustache is magnified by his helmet's face shield so that it looks like a cat is sitting on his face. He swings a full-brimmed hat overtop his helmet, and train E starts off slowly for tunnel E.

My basket is spacious because I'm short. The man in front of me, who looks about six feet, two inches and two hundred pounds or so, looks cramped, knees to chest.

"Hey, neighbor," I shout as our train starts to move.

He looks over his shoulder. He nods. "Kevin."

"Dana."

He nods again and then looks ahead.

The surface of Phoebe is rock. It seems impossible, but most of it is seamless, as if one big chunk of melted ore was shot out of Saturn's volcanoes. No sediment. No sand. No small rocks. Just smooth, jagged, and ugly. Once you crack that surface, though, it's a mess of sandy stone with veins of lithium, copper, and steel. Train C is a lithium vein line.

The lithium veins are almost-straight lines pancaked in large chunks of granite.

"Race?" Kevin swings his pickaxe at the wall.

I swing. "You're on."

Thirty minutes later, our buckets are filled. My bucket's green light glowed first. "Ha!"

"You are strong for being so little."

My head comes up to his chest. "I'll show you little." I hoist my axe.

"No. . . . No need for that." He sits against the wall. "Nothing to do but wait."

"We could help the neighbors." I point to the woman beyond him and the guy on the other side of me. "Neighborly thing to do, yeah?"

"Maybe. Pay's the same though." He nods at his bucket. "By the bucket, yeah?"

"Suit yourself, Kevin." I walk down the line. "Hey, neighbor."

The guy stops swinging. "Nicolas."

"Dana." I point to the wall. "Can I help?"

He eyes me. "What would I owe you?" He takes another swing at the wall. Chunks of stone crumble to the ground.

"Be my neighbor."

He shrugs. "I don't know what you mean, but I could use the help. This rock is stubborn." His swing only produces small rocks and a bit of sand.

Ten minutes later, his bucket is full and he is resting. I move down the line. I meet Janice, Rupert, Nagal, and Cooper before we get the signal that the train is full.

I stand against the striped wall with my axe pressed to my chest. Cooper is smiling. As the caboose passes, the pedaler takes his hands off the steering bars to make not one, but three lewd gestures.

"You know the pedaler?"

"I sat at the wrong table this morning. Good talking with you, Cooper. I hope we can be neighbors." I head back to my section of the wall. Everyone is resting with suits powered down. If they lose power during your shift, you can't complete your work. You'll owe for lost productivity and for the assistance to get you out of the tunnel and back to your bunk—it's expensive. I just don't care. It's not like I'm ever going to be able to afford to leave this rock. That's why I've got to do this neighbor shit. I've got to make a life here I want. I've got nothing else, and what I want is to have a few friends and, I think, be a pedaler.

I picture the silly pages of that Mr. Rogers book. It was hidden under my mattress. I wonder whose it was. Was it a mother remembering her kid's favorite story? I don't know. The poem-song thing at the beginning is just so true. I want neighbors. I need neighbors. What the hell happened to neighbors? Even on Earth, I didn't know the people living next door, let alone down the hall from me. Now, I don't even know Sarah, my roommate.

I fill the second bucket quickly. Instead of helping my neighbors, I head all the way down the line until I reach the back of the train.

"Dana."

"Ivan."

I pat a tire. "So, who do I talk to?"

"Wats is boss." He blinks really slow. "When pedaler dies, there is race. Winner is next pedaler."

"I want to race."

"None dead." He looks confused. "None dead, no race."

"When was the last race?"

"Fifteen cycles." A green light blinks on. "Got to go." He releases the brake. "You not worry about pedaling. None dead. You woman." Ivan hooks his thumb. "Go pound wall."

Three more loads and the day's done. I met people. I think that Mr. Rogers would be proud. Not grumpy Lady Elaine Fairchilde who wants to be left alone. However, by the end of the book, she's ready to have a friend. She was just afraid to meet new people. I think that's the message that I needed to hear. I'll be happier with friends, neighbors.

When I walk into the mess hall for dinner, I get a few waves to sit at various tables. I want to so badly, but I plunk down next to Wats. "I want to race."

Ivan says, "I tell you."

Wats laughs.

"I want to race."

"I can see that," says Wats. He scratches his ear. "Ivan's right. No dead. No race. You're a woman." He holds up his hand before I can protest. "But, a race could be . . . profitable. You find me seven ladies, and we'll have us a ladies' competition." He smiles. "Make a night of it. Betting, drinking, fucking." He chews his mustache. "I got to clear it up the chain, but I think they'll go for it."

"I can do that." I get up from the table. Take a breath. I can meet more new people. I make a round of the room, sitting, chatting, getting to know my neighbors. It takes so long that I miss dinner, but I find six others. I put the list on the table in front of Wats. "Me, River, Sarah, Heather, Jane, Michelle, and Advika. Winner gets half the pot."

"Quarter."

"Third."

Wats points up at the deck. "They'll want half. Winner and I split the other half, so a quarter or nothing." He folds his arms.

The lights blink three times. It's time to head to the bunks. Everyone starts off for their dorms. Women through one door, men through another. Couples through a third. Couples with kids through a fourth. I've heard that the family wing is nice. Kids are encouraged. New workers indentured from the womb.

As the lights dim, I ask Sarah, "Want to be my neighbor?"

"What?"

"You know, friends."

"Why didn't you just say friends?"

"I don't know. So, do you?"

"Sure. You got me into the race already. So, yeah. Friends."

"Good night, neighbor."

•　　•　　•

The race course is checked three times. Mr. Dunken walked each tunnel and inspected the weight and fullness of the buckets. Setup took half the day. Our day off. To make the race happen, we all put in a few hours filling the trains for free. Mr. Dunken and the other managers must be laughing.

Wats laughs as he explains the race to us *ladies*.

"If you can't get started, flip this switch here. It'll tell us you quit. Trains need two men during the work cycle. When we race, there is just one man. The record was set by Henderson. He's long dead, the bastard. Somehow, he got his train to the refinery in under fifteen minutes. Next best time is Ivan's at twenty-five."

"If one of us beats Ivan's time, I want the winner to be next in line for pedaler."

"Done," says a voice.

Wats's head snaps over his shoulder so fast I thought it would fall off. Mr. Dunken and two other of management's finest stand behind him. "That's my call!"

"Productivity is productivity." They walk away.

"Was this the plan?" He looks like he wants to spit behind his face shield. "I choose who pedals. Not you, me!" Wats places boxes in front of each of us. The box in front of me, in dark letters says, "Dana, 20 to 1." I can see only two of the others. Sarah's, "5 to 1." River, "2 to 1."

Wats calls, "twenty minutes. Bets close in twenty minutes."

The crowd hurried by, dropping bets in the boxes. Cooper goes to drop a bet in my box, but I bend and catch it. "You sure?"

Cooper looks confused. "I think you'll win." He puts his bet in the box.

I shrug. Good a bet as any, I guess. I want to win. I had a bike on Earth. I loved that thing. I rode to work every day. That bike was more than transportation; it was a friend until it was stolen. I never got another one. I didn't have the money.

"Racers, to your trains." Wats is nothing short of a showman. He calls out our names and train tunnels. He gets the crowd cheering for us as we walk down the lines.

As I enter tunnel B, it gets real quiet. I can't hear the crowd. I can hear my heart and my breath, but that's about it. I find the four-wheeler and climb in. I adjust the seat so I can reach the pedals. I remove the brake. There are five gears. I look at the cog and the shifter. It's in the climbing gear. So, I'm set. I wait. I get a feel for the seating and the handles, which are at my legs like a true recumbent. Strange. I guess some of the trains are different.

The light flashes on the dash. "Shit." That's the go signal. I thought there would have been a countdown or some noise. Not just quiet then go. My legs burn as my back presses into the seat and I pull up on the handles. The train moves forward half a wheel but rocks back on me two wheels in length. *Damn. Let's go, Dana! Push!*

Even with the suit's power, I can't get it moving. Something is wrong. I put the brake in place and run down the line, checking the wheels. There! A piece of ore wedged under a tire. Can't think about this being sabotage. I just got to get going. I make a lap around the back end of the train, finding two more rocks. I get back to the front and go. The train starts to move. It's slow. How did anyone do this in less than fifteen minutes? Henderson must have been a beast.

I've finally got enough momentum that I can shift. If I push any harder, I'm going to bust my teeth. Everything hurts, but I'm going to make it. I'm going to get this train to the refinery. I'm going to do it. I don't look at the clock. I don't dare. It's been forever. It's been too long. Will there even be anyone waiting for me at the finish line?

I see my parents. My dad says, "Loser. Get a real job. Get out of the house. You're twenty-seven for fuck's sake." My mother says, "Good girls don't go into space." I went anyway. I got a job. I got out of the house. My heart is pounding so hard. Am I dying?

I see tears on the signature page of my recruitment papers. Mine? My mom's? The neighbor, Ben Collins's? He had been good to me. When I needed extra money for something stupid, he always had a little for me. He bought me a dress for the high school winter formal when I was fourteen. His daughter had died in a car crash with her drunk boyfriend. Afterwards, he kinda adopted me. Said I could live in his basement if my parents were done with me, just don't go to Phoebe.

Screaming, the train's on the flat. I shift again and again. I'm going so fast, I can't see. I can't hear people shouting, "Brake!"

I see Ivan. He's waving. I pedal harder. The sound of metal on stone is worse than chalk on a school board. The next thing that I know is that I'm laying on the ground and the world is spinning. Wats is standing over me yelling. I can't make out what he says.

• • •

Sarah is shaking me.

The room comes into focus. I hurt. I look for a toilet. My stomach contents are on the floor.

"You're an idiot." She punches me in the shoulder. "Could've killed a lot more people with that stunt of yours. Management's pissed."

"More. . . ." I may need to vomit again.

"Shit. You don't know." She put a hand on my shoulder. "You crushed Ivan against the wall and breached the refinery."

I feel another wave of nausea.

The door clicks open and admits Mr. Dunken and two guards.

Mr. Dunken points to me.

The guards start to roll the bed out the door, and I grab hold of Sarah. "Who won?" My grip slips.

"Advika."

My eyes flutter. I may pass out. "What was her time?"

"Twenty-four minutes and ten seconds. She's replacing Ivan."

Consciousness slips away.

·   ·   ·

When I wake, I'm in a cell. I can just make out someone to my left through the bars. I ask, "Want to be my neighbor?"

SO YOU WANT TO BE A VÉLO-ARCHIVIST?

Grace Gorski

If you love books and biking long distances, the vélo-archives might have the career for you!

—Vélo-Archivist Informational Pamphlet

. . . .

Aster glanced over the vélo-archivist pamphlet on her tablet one last time before stowing it in her bike's saddlebag. She couldn't believe she was finally doing this.

"Aster Anston, vélo-archivist," she muttered to herself. The title felt weighty on her tongue every time she said it. And soon, it would actually be hers. Never mind that Aster hated biking long distances. At least, that was what she told herself when she reread that part of the pamphlet. Surely not all vélo-archivists biked *long* distances regularly.

Career Day had been two months ago, and, ever since, Aster had been counting down the days until the end of school. Until today.

Aster mounted her bike and set off, paying no mind to the school building she was leaving behind. Instead, her eyes landed on the town's archive across the street from the school and directly adjacent to the library. When Aster was a kid, she was taught that putting the archive next to the library was in homage to the days when books were housed in libraries. Aster knew the library as the place to get seeds for the garden, tools for the home, party decorations, and costumes. Libraries were for sharing materials. Archives were for sharing knowledge. But not every community was big enough to house its own archive. Vélo-archivists were critical in making sure that every community, no matter its size, had access to knowledge. Aster smiled to herself. Soon, she would play that critical role. First stop: home, to grab her bag and say goodbye.

·   ·   ·

We bike from place to place, usually between towns and out to more remote communities. . . . At each destination, the vélo-archivist records stories and collects any personal records or correspondence the residents offer. Vélo-archivists also repair paper books as needed, especially in areas without a permanent archive.

·   ·   ·

The ride from Woodmoss School to Aster's home was short, but it took twice as long as usual. It seemed as though everyone in Woodmoss was outside celebrating the class of 2250. Aster's parents had asked if she wanted a party, but Aster said no. Aster's mom had nodded and returned to her puzzle, but Aster's zaza had looked crestfallen.

Aster had given them a hug. "I'm sorry, Zaza," Aster said. "It's just . . . the ride from Woodmoss to Eden is long, and if I miss orientation at the National Archives, I'll have to wait months for the next one!"

Zaza rubbed Aster's back. "I know, sweetheart," they said. They knew more than anyone how long Aster had been awed by the vélo-archivist who visited Woodmoss quarterly. More than once they had caught child-Aster attempting to eavesdrop on the sharing of one story or another. They sighed. "I just wanted to celebrate the closing of one chapter and the opening of another."

Aster was quiet for a moment, lulled by the rhythmic back rub. "What if we have a nice dinner the day before I leave? But just us. That sounds like the perfect celebration to me." She'd moved back half a step to look Zaza in the eye.

Zaza smiled. "That sounds wonderful."

Now, as Aster braked in front of her house, she could see her parents waiting outside for her. She dismounted and hurried to them for hugs and more than a few tears.

"Are you ready?" Mom asked. Aster nodded.

"One more thing before you go," Zaza said. Before Aster could respond, they disappeared into the house.

Aster turned to her mom, one eyebrow raised.

"You'll see," Mom said with a smile.

Zaza emerged a moment later, holding a can of orange paint. Aster frowned. "What's this?"

Zaza grinned. "I've done my research. I know that all vélo-archivists ride orange bicycles. I know you need to get going. But I wanted to send you on your way with some orange paint, and maybe a few symbolic orange patches on your bike."

Aster felt a smile to match Zaza's spread across her face. She looked back at her silver bicycle. "Yes. Let's."

•   •   •

Even if you've never interacted with a vélo-archivist, odds are you've seen them riding around. Have you ever seen an orange bike with a small gray trailer attached to the back? That is a vélo-archive.

•   •   •

An hour later, Aster was finally ready to go. Her silver bike now sported three stripes of orange, and the remaining paint was nestled in one pannier, next to her sleeping bag. Aster guessed she had about three hours before it would be too dark to ride safely on unfamiliar roads.

Aster double-checked that her belongings were all safely stowed. She switched her tablet into riding mode and then stowed it in its pouch on top of her rear rack.

Aster gave one last hug to each of her parents. "Ping us when you stop for the night," Mom said. Aster nodded.

"And when you get going in the morning," Zaza added.

Aster rolled her eyes even as she smiled. "I'll ping you every time there's a meaningful stop."

"Good," Zaza said.

One last hug, and Aster's parents went back inside the house. This, too, had been discussed before. Aster knew her departure would be delayed if her parents stayed outside until she was out of sight.

With her parents inside, Aster mounted her bike and pushed away from her childhood home.

•   •   •

> By riding from city to town to remote commune, vélo-archivists ensure that everyone has a chance for their story to be heard. Our work is vital in reinforcing the connections between individuals, their communities, and humanity at large.

•   •   •

The streets of Woodmoss were emptier now than they had been when Aster had first left school. She guessed that many families were enjoying end-of-school celebrations, even for those who hadn't graduated. Those who weren't celebrating were likely squeezing in another hour or so of work, maybe in Woodmoss's gardens or at one of the community kitchens. She wondered what kind of celebrations were taking place in the teachers' housing.

Aster encountered only a handful of other bicycles between her home and the eastern border of Woodmoss. Everyone wished Aster good luck, even those who didn't know exactly where she was going.

As soon as Aster left Woodmoss proper, road traffic decreased to almost nothing. Aster checked her watch—five thirty. Dinner time for most. Aster would stop and eat when it was too dark to ride.

·   ·   ·

Like other archivists, vélo-archivists are guardians of words. Each vélo-archivist is assigned a route that is to be completed over a certain length of time, usually a week or a month, with an equal amount of time spent off between circuits of that route.

·   ·   ·

Just before sunset, Aster reached a roadside bike shelter. She was officially farther from Woodmoss than she had ever biked on her own before, although she had vague memories of stopping at this shelter on a family camping trip when she was a kid. Already, her legs ached from a pace more grueling than she was used to. It was the one thing that had given her pause when making her decision on Career Day: Aster wasn't fond of the long, exploratory rides that many of her peers enjoyed once they were old enough to leave Woodmoss without adult supervision. Aster much preferred riding in familiar territory. *But*, she'd told herself, *a vélo-archivist route will become familiar territory in time.* And surely a little discomfort was a price worth paying for the honor of hearing and preserving the stories of others. Aster could think of no task more important.

Aster parked her bike in the shelter and rolled her sleeping bag out next to it. From her bags, Aster grabbed her tablet and a nutrition bar. While eating, Aster pinged her parents to let them know she was safe and settled. Before long, she had settled in for the night and drifted into the sound rest of a well-worked body.

• • •

The National Archives offers a training program for potential archivists. All trainee archivists learn about handling fragile books, basic book repair, book storage guidelines, and more. Those in the vélo-archivist concentration get additional training in maintaining the archive trailer, navigating seldom-used roads in poor weather, guidelines for interviews, and more. The program takes about two years to complete, including a six-month apprenticeship. Like most workforce training programs, it is tuition-free.

• • •

Aster woke early the next morning, while the air was still cool and damp. According to the route she'd planned, she had four hours of riding to get to Eden and to the National Archives. Although she hadn't ever been to Eden before, Aster knew the route was straightforward. Still a bit stiff from yesterday's ride, Aster regarded the distance that still lay between her and the National Archives as her first test: forty or fifty miles in a day wasn't unusual for a vélo-archivist, and often they would only stay in one place for a day or two.

As Aster rode along, she passed several merchants hauling large wagons behind their bicycles but no vélo-archivists. She wondered if she would see a single orange bicycle on the road to

Eden. The scenery around Aster shifted seamlessly from woods to wild fields to cultivated farmland and back again. Here and there, signs at intersections indicated communities that Aster passed by without stopping.

After two hours of riding, every small incline made Aster's eyes fill with tears. Her breathing grew more labored with every mile. She hadn't yet stopped for a break longer than ten minutes for fear of losing her momentum. Old doubts bubbled up in her mind: Aster remembered taking to cycling later than her friends, her desire for shorter excursions. But each doubt also brought to mind a story shared with or learned from a vélo-archivist: city folk during the transition away from cars who mastered biking in heels and suits, and her own story of when she finally grew to love her own bike. She reminded herself that she would get stronger over time.

Finally, three and a half hours in, Aster saw Eden looming on the horizon. Aster marveled at buildings so large that she could see them from so far away. No one built skyscrapers anymore, but the people of Eden used the ones that were already there until they were no longer safe.

·   ·   ·

The climate crisis in the twenty-first century destroyed much of our written documentation. . . . Most of what we lost was personal: diaries, journals, letters. In short, we lost the voice of the people. So, while general archivists continue to catalog and maintain our literature, manuals, and other written materials, the vélo-archivists are concerned with stories.

·   ·   ·

At last, Aster reached a large, imposing building on one end of a bustling square. The ride into Eden had been a blur, so focused was Aster on her destination. Now that she stopped and looked around, Aster was struck by the sheer number of people around her. There were more people in that one square than she had ever seen at one time in Woodmoss.

Letters carved above the entrance to the building read National Archives. Near the left corner of the archives, Aster saw a small fleet of orange bicycles—the vélo-archives. Aster locked her bike to the public rack closest to the vélo-archives.

On foot, Aster returned to the entrance to the National Archives. She squared her shoulders and took a deep breath. Then, she walked towards her future.

·   ·   ·

Help save our stories. Become a vélo-archivist.

AI-SAG

Julie Brooks

WELCOME, INTERSTELLAR VELOCIPEDIST!

S o, here you are, standing at a cosmic crossroads. You have shredded and screamed through gnarl for the past two centuries to get here, consumed an inordinate amount of mediocre coffee, and pondered the meaning of life without coming to any substantial, satiating conclusions. Trailed and trampled daily by those radium-powered orbs piloted by radioactive kneebiters seeking salvation in the privacy of their own space cars, you've been forced to pitch a line through some seriously distorted ion trails around the off-camber section of Orion. Left feeling like you've been pedaling squares through thick layers of interstellar dust particles bigger than the bearings in that grunt bike your cousin rides and frustrated by being constantly compelled to take the long way home through the Virgo Cluster to avoid the rush hour, you have arrived at an intersection of warp trails, with a very nice coffee shop.

Now you have a choice to make: you can continue rambling through and around the flocks of flying cars crowding your beloved Cosmos, perhaps even try to stop the squeezing out of cycle-pilots minding their own business. Or, you could keep' pedaling, out into the wild, wondrous, exciting, and possibly excruciating Zone of Avoidance that lies beyond the Milky Way. Whatever you decide—and certainly there's always something in-between—the AI[1]-SAG,[2] a catalog of useful tools and tales for

---

1 Artificial Intelligence
2 Support and Gear: a twentieth-century concept signifying an individual,

the interstellar, trip-taking, java-sipping velocipedist, is here to help you on your daily or never-ending commute.

The AI-SAG is a communications implant (or "com" as we refer to it in the business), developed by a far-flung faction of brilliant, reflective, and jovial female bike mechanics. Calling themselves the Pedal Wrench Gang, this group of probing, peaceable, Cosmos-preserving, and self-proclaimed "guardians of the intergalactic wheel" created the AI-SAG as a response to the troubling trend of velocipedes and galactic scooters being crowded and crammed out of even the most protected cycle tracks by high-octane flying cars piloted by self-absorbed interplanetary day-trippers.

The implant, a small microchip (akin to the twentieth-century cochlear implant), is inserted just under the epidermis on the mastoid process and connected to the cochlear nerve. With a light touch to the skin covering the implant behind the ear, users can access their personalized Remote Artificial Intelligence Assistant (RAIA) for coffee-finding support and recommendations about the most cutting-edge gear available to hyperspace pedalers looking to navigate the crowded Cosmos with discretion and determination.

Below is a sampling of the repository available to the intrepid two-wheeled traveler, including a brief explanation of our cosmically patented Galaxial Coffee Positioning System (GCPS): today's answer to the age-old question, "Where can I get a great cup o' jo?"

---

oftentimes driving a support vehicle, who provided tools and repairs, food, first aid, and sometimes a ride to cyclists on long journeys.

GEAR

The Multitudinous XS-Pedelex Booster

The Multitudinous XS-Pedelex Booster is an amazing new system for pedaling enormous interstellar distances in no time (though not quite hyperspeed) without all the tedious fooling around in uninteresting, regional dimensions to which most Milky Way residents escape for holidays and other vital vacations. Designed by the Simmons triplets—Winnie, Binnie, and Nell of the Trappist-1 solar system (a quiet, watery system of seven stars inhabited by highly intelligent mystics who have little tolerance for idle chatter)—and very distant granddaughters of Michelle Simmons (that no-nonsense, twentieth-century quantum physicist known for her creation of the field of quantum electronics), the Multitudinous XS-Pedelex Booster combines a simple battery pack fit snugly inside the crank arm of your bike with the wirelessly connected, cosmic-patented Pedelex pedal (available in clipless or flat). The Multitudinous XS-Pedelex Booster is powered by a torque transducer that detects when pressure is applied with the plantar plate in the pedaler's foot to the pedals in a gravity-free environment. Once pressure is applied, the Booster kicks into gear, sending the rider soaring through space for the next 47 minutes.

The Point-of-View Pump

The Point-of-View Pump does exactly what its name suggests. It was discovered by Deep Clean—a short, straight-backed, red-haired Serenian velocipede racer—during the degreasing session of a pretty nasty, mucked-up crankset on a bike resembling a Bianchi Strada Italia from way before the Jetsonian Age.

Deep Clean worked for an oblivious, snarling, boxy-shouldered Venetian named Minion Able. He was a jerk, a complete kneebiter, haranguing and harassing Deep Clean every chance he could get.

One afternoon, while working on that mucked-up crankset, the silver shaft of a vintage-looking hand pump hanging from the top tube by a ragged piece of Velcro—a tool and material Deep Clean hadn't seen for eons—seemed to dangle a bit while Deep Clean was spraying galaxiodegradable solution onto the cassette. No rhyme or reason to it. It just dangled, dancing back and forth like it was swinging to the Betelgeusian Helmet Dance. Minion, being his characteristically annoying self, blasted through the door, nitpicking and complaining about Deep Clean's wrenching prowess.

"Why are you working on that vintage piece of . . . ?" Minion trailed off.

"Because it's here. That's what I do," Deep Clean shot back without looking up. Deep Clean knew Minion was insecure and jealous, trying to get a rise out of her, and she whispered to herself, "You know, those BarMart bikes you bought to 'fix up' and resell to unsuspecting customers are pieces of near-junk." Minion overheard her and persisted in berating her.

"What do you know? Those Cruisers are beautiful," he boasted. "They could be the best, you know, *the best* bikes. Look at how gorgeous they are."

"You know, Able," Deep Clean interrupted, continuing to spray the cassette, careful not to get any of the degreasing solution on the hub so as to avoid dissolving the grease in the bearings, "you really should just donate those pieces of near-junk to the kids beyond the Virgo Void. Give them a chance to work on 'em and learn some wrenching skills."

"Nonsense," Minion shouted, turning away from Deep Clean. "I can fix them up and sell them for millions!"

Just then, the pump broke loose from the Velcro, disconnected from the top tube, and took to the air, twirling and twisting, until it finally hit the ground. As it bounced arhythmically across the wooden floor, the shaft of the pump spread open, then closed, spread open, then closed again, as if it were pumping itself. When it finally came to a stop, hitting the front of Minion's left foot, Minion's attitude changed instantly: "You know Deep Clean, you're right," he said, turning back around and looking Deep Clean square in the eye. "I've been an ass," he submitted. "Maybe I will donate those bikes to the Virgo Void on the other side of the blue moon. I don't need the money."

That's the beauty of the Point-of-View Pump. When you point it at someone and pump it a few times, they instantly see things from your point of view.

Blip-o-Zap Blaster

Every pedaler in the Galaxy has one of those days when some speedy, spaced-out RacSpakShi driver seems to come out of nowhere, whizzes around to the left, then abruptly turns right, cutting the pedaler off, yells obscenities, then speeds away while flipping 'em the bird. Well, with a Blip-o-Zap Blaster clipped onto your handlebars,[3] you'll be ready to get even. Unlike its predecessor, the raygun-resembling Kill-o-Zap Gun, the Blip-o-Zap is not all that evil and won't make people miserable. The Blip-o-Zap Blaster is a smallish 6100-lumen LED bike light with two buttons on the top. When you need some extra light while you're out there exploring the Cosmos, simply depress the blue button and, *voila!*, you'll light up like the parking lot at Milliways. If, however, you have a run-in with a seemingly insane space motorist, you need only

---

3 For your convenience, the Blip-o-Zap Blaster comes with an adapter kit for attaching it directly to your coffee-cup holder should you be running out of space on your handlebars.

to depress the green button and watch as that not-so-friendly glumbell disappears into infinity.

In actuality, there's no real blasting taking place, and you won't be annihilating anyone. You will, however, be inconveniencing your fevered friend by sending them back in time, to a place and moment when they had to make a difficult choice, drink cold coffee, and listen to the Dentrassis—that unruly tribe of large, yellow, bug-eyed gourmands that predated the now completely self-obsessed subspecies, the Neo-Dentrassis—launch into long tirades about the unfairness of the Cosmos even when things were going fairly well. Your rage-filled culprit will certainly need to know something about the fabric of space-time, and it wouldn't hurt if they had some experience with Mobius strips. But, hey, that won't be your problem.

Sub-Ubiqui-Cop Direct-o-Chine

It's a mouthful to say, so best not to say the word out loud more than once a day. The Sub-Ubiqui-Cop Direct-o-Chine is a glorious tool for the interstellar velocipedist new to pedaling the Galaxy. In short, despite its longish name, the Sub-Ubiqui-Cop Direct-o-Chine is a small purplish device with a large yellow light—about the size of a late-model activity tracker that humans used to wear on their wrists when they went running in the Alps on Earth—that monitors the whereabouts of other pedalers in the outer solar system (those in the inner solar system use something completely different). It is particularly useful for those who are not yet familiar with the region outside of the Horsehead Nebula as its light blinks rapidly when other pedalers are within a quarter of a light year away. It also has a unique blinking pattern when it detects the presence of a dwarf planet with at least three coffee shop options within range of a week's worth of pedaling, offering the velocipedist a plethora of appealing opportunities for exploration and caffeine-quenching encounters.

You can wear the Sub-Ubiqui-Cop Direct-o-Chine on your wrist, but most pedalers wear it on their right ankles. This way they can protect their dark gray flannel parachute pants from getting caught in the sprockets—though, most pedalers have a bashguard for such things. The Sub-Ubiqui-Cop Direct-o-Chine is a trendy and tantalizing piece of technology that can all but guarantee the interstellar velocipedist new to pedaling around and beyond the Milky Way Galaxy will look and feel like a sophisticated and seasoned explorer.

The Boomer Hammock

Finally, the most massively useful item for any interstellar velocipedist is the Boomer Hammock. Conceived by the Bitpouch sisters, who were pedaling around the Galaxy way before the Simmons triplets, the Boomer Hammock is a significant and sensible investment. A seven-by-four-foot sheet of cytoplasmic membrane particles, this hammock is equipped with two crystalline quickdraw mechanisms at each end so that you can string your hammock between two tree-like multicellular structures on exoplanets all over the Galaxy. If you prefer to lie in the fetal position on a flat mattress on a dwarf planet, the Boomer Hammock provides great protection from dew and mist on some of the swampier stars. It would behoove you not to attach the ends of the hammock on the gray tree-like multicellular structures on Mercury, however, or lay prone facing the sky. Remember, as the sun rises and sets over the massive metallic core of that swift-moving planet, one can experience the distinct feeling of hopelessness and long-lasting lethargy after laying in the extreme heat of the day and then curling up during intensely icy nights.

The Boomer Hammock is also a wonderful blanket for those random comfortably cool nights when the Mimas moon turns "blue," or when laying atop the Caloris Basin. It can be used as a sail for warm, lazy evenings drifting along the River of Stars or as a straightjacket, wrapped around one of those annoyingly accomplished and enlightened Martian monks when they've driven you crazy with their maddeningly unresponsive silence. If you bring along two largish U-shaped pole supports (sold separately), the Boomer can be turned into a tent, shading you from the bright, sweltering sun, for example, shining over the subtropical coastline of Ursa Minor Beta.

Most important of all of its uses however, is its immense psychological value. Especially in the presence of a spulg (noninterstellar velocipedist), if an interstellar pedaler dons a Boomer Hammock at just the right moment, the spulg will unthinkingly assume that the pedaler has an incredible amount of experience and expertise and that they must, of course, be in possession of two extra tubes, canisters of air and oil, four tire irons, self-cleaning rags, a collapsible coffee mug, a washcloth, floss, and an oxygen tank for high-altitude pedaling. This prepared pedaler would not be someone a spulg would want to mess with since they would assume that such an intrepid interstellar velocipedist, a woman willing to pedal the length of the Galaxy at speeds both slow and steadfast to find the best coffee, a woman equipped to sleep on anything and under any star system (even on Kepler-1b, where an extremely low geometric albedo—not libido—reflects less light than a piece of coal), a woman who would struggle in both heat and chill to get to her next adventure, is surely a woman to be reckoned with!

Galaxial Coffee Positioning System

The Galaxial Coffee Positioning System (GCPS)[4] is our cosmically patented answer to locating intergalactic coffee outposts that cater to your unique interstellar trip-taking tastes. The GCPS can be customized and calibrated to the preferred grind (PG), desired quantity (DQ), and daily coffee intake (DCI) of each unique user. Once RAIA is installed, and an interface is established, she will prompt you to input your coffee specifications.[5] Immediately following your input, RAIA, attuned to your peculiar palate and preference, will be capable of making suggestions for intergalactic coffee outposts throughout and beyond the Milky Way Galaxy.

For more information about the AI-SAG implant, please visit a Pedal Wrench Gang representative at one of our Cosmos Cyclery locations listed below:

Mars Shop, Sunday through Friday, 9:00 a.m. to 6:00 p.m.

Trappist-1 system, fourth planet, Saturday & most Sundays, 6:00 a.m. to 9:00 p.m.

So long, and thanks for the pour-over!

---

4 As a special offer to first time users of the AI-SAG, Cosmic Café—based on Antares, with shops floating around Eres, Ceres, Betelgeuse and soon to be located in a shadow plaza in the Zone of Avoidance—will provide interstellar pedalers with a one-kilogram bag of dark roast Milky Way-OUT! Instant Espresso: "Dude, for those moments when you need a boost in your biking boots!"

5 Coffee specifications can be modified once daily for the life of your RAIA.

CONTRIBUTORS

Aaron M. Wilson's fiction is a strange mixture of science fiction, urban fantasy, bike mechanics, tattoos, yoga, and environmental activism. If new to his work, start with *Tree Bomber and Other Stories* or the first volume of *Bikes in Space*.

With their fluffy cat, Sgt. Quark Amaya McFluffers, **Aidan Zingler** explores reality while balanced precariously between the days of yesterday and the tremors of the present. Aidan is a void of genderlessness that they ascribe to the stars, their body composed of star guts. They write science fiction, poetry, nonfiction essays, and sometimes a blog post on their website: ReshapingReality.org. They also write fiction as TheBirdWrites on Archives of Our Own.

Allison Bannister is a cartoonist and comics scholar, interested in unconventional materials, multimodal rhetoric, and composition practices. Her comics tend toward the fantastical, engaging fairy tales, mythology, and magical elements to tell stories with a human core. You can find her work in various anthologies or online at https://BasicTelepathy.com.

Annie Carl is a high-functioning physically disabled woman who never did learn how to ride a bike. When not writing, she can be found reading massive quantities of nerdy books, pole dancing, knitting, and hanging with her friends and family. She is the author of three books— *My Tropey Life: How Pop Culture Stereotypes Make Disabled Lives Harder*, *Nebula Vibrations*, and *Soul Jar: Thirty-One Fantastical Tales by Disabled Authors*. Her dad is an enthusiastic cyclist and is quite proud of Annie's story.

Cherise Fong travels around Japan with her bicycle whenever possible, seeking out remote cat islands, craggy capes, and alternate pilgrimage paths across the archipelago. She writes quirky microfictions when not possessed by her one-eyed black-and-white bobtailed demon cat.

Dawn Vogel has been reading and telling stories since she was very young, and she's glad to have had many fiction books as her guide. She lives in Seattle with her husband, author Jeremy Zimmerman, and their herd of cats. Visit her: HistoryThatNeverWas.com

Elizabeth Frazier (she/her) is a writer, editor, and perpetual dream machine based in the Midwest. If she's not at her desk, she's probably at the library or giving her sisters' tiny humans too much sugar. You can find her at https://ElizabethAFrazier.com or on Instagram at @ ElizabethMakesPoems.

Elly Blue is the editor of this series and spends a lot of time biking around town looking for discarded wood to build shelves out of and contemplating how publishing might change in the future. She lives with her partner, dog, and a small fleet of cargo bikes in Portland, Oregon.

Grace Gorski (she/her) is a queer writer, cyclist, and early childhood educator living in St. Louis, Missouri. She is a graduate of Hollins University. Grace probably spends too much time snuggling her dog while playing Animal Crossing.

Gretchin Lair extends her deepest appreciation to Janna Levin & Carlo Rovelli, who each write the most beautiful books about the hardest sciences. She is equally grateful to Brian Tillotson, who encouraged and verified the science in this story. If you want to know more about how to survive a black hole, you can contact Gretchin at gretchin@ ScarletStarStudios.com.

Julie Brooks is an intergenre writer, interspiritual minister and guide, and the chief executive pedaler of https://SacredCycling.com. She has a keen interest in contemplative practices across the wisdom traditions and is currently working on setting some of those practices onto the saddle in her forthcoming book, *Back to the Hub: InterSpiritual Practices for Sacred Cycling*. Blessed be the wonder of wandering the world on a wheel!

By day, **Kathryn Reilly** helps students investigate words' power; at night, she reads retold myths and spins new ones. Enjoy poetic adventures in *Shadow Atlas: Dark Landscape of the Americas*, *The Willow Tree Swing*, *Blink Ink*, and *Whiptail Journal* and fiction with Tree and Stone, Elly Blue Publishing, and Oddity Prodigy Productions. Her rescue mutts Savvie and Roxy Razzamatazz hear the stories first. She often writes in a treehouse. Twitter: @KateCanWrite

Kiera Jessica Bane (she/her) is an autistic transwoman from London, England. When she's not riding her bike, she can be found writing, fixing bikes, or sketching. She has the word "Broccoli" tattooed across her fingers and really hopes this writing business pays off. She can be praised/harassed on Instagram @Tranzig_666.

L.Y. Gu is an Asian American technology analyst working in Virginia who writes short stories and loves stories in all their forms.

Mariah Southworth is a writer of horror, fantasy, and science fiction from the northwestern United States. Her short stories have appeared in *Humans Wanted* by Cuppatea Publications, *Bubble Off Plumb* by Feral Cat Publishers, *Monsters in Space!* by Dragon's Roost Press, and *Supernatural Horror Short Stories* by Flame Tree Publishing. Her self-published children's books, *Lydia! No Lying!*, *24 Scary Poems for Scary Kids*, and *I Am A. . .* are available on Amazon. For more about Mariah Southworth, visit her website MariahSouthworth.com.

Remy Chartier is a queer and trans author, hailing from New Hampshire. For two years, they taught a class at San Francisco State University on transformative fiction and the importance of uncensored creativity in an increasingly capitalist society. Above all else, they identify as a teller of stories. Their work can be found in *The Ana* quarterly arts zine, *Decoded Pride*, and at other small presses.

Summer Jewel Keown lives in Indianapolis where she writes speculative fiction and lives that environmental-nonprofit life. You can read more of her stories in other volumes of *Bikes in Space*, including *Bikes Not Rockets* and *C.A.T.S.: Cycling across Time in Space*. She is the coeditor of *Non-stalgia: A Fiction Anthology*. She has also authored the sapphic romance collection *Heartlocked Witches of the Midwest* and novels *Painted Over* and *False Starts & Artichoke Hearts* under the pen name Sofi Keren. Say hi at MedusaFish.com.

CREATE THE WORLD YOU WANT TO SEE AT MICROCOSM.PUB

C.A.T.S.
CYCLING ACROSS TIME AND SPACE
11 FEMINIST SCIENCE FICTION AND FANTASY STORIES ABOUT BICYCLING AND CATS
EDITED BY
ELLY BLUE

TRANS-GALACTIC BIKE RIDE
FEMINIST BICYCLE SCIENCE FICTION STORIES OF TRANSGENDER AND NONBINARY ADVENTURERS
LYDIA ROGUE

BIKES NOT ROCKETS
INTERSECTIONAL FEMINIST BICYCLE SCIENCE FICTION ROCKETS
EDITED BY
ELLY BLUE

DRAGON BIKE
FANTASTICAL STORIES OF BICYCLING, FEMINISM, AND DRAGONS
ELLY BLUE

SUBSCRIBE!

For as little as $15/month, you can support a small, independent publisher and get every book that we publish—delivered to your doorstep!

www.**Microcosm.Pub/BFF**

PESTS UNITE!

MICROCOSMPUBLISHING.COM

MORE FEMINIST BICYCLE SCIENCE FICTION:

BIKE TOPIA
FEMINIST BICYCLE SIENCE FICTION STORIES IN EXTREME FUTURES
EDITED BY
ELLY BLUE

BIKES IN SPACE
Volume II
More feminist science fiction
Edited by Elly Blue

BIKES IN SPACE
a feminist science fiction anthology

BICYCLES & BROOMSTICKS
FANTASTICAL FEMINIST STORIES ABOUT WITCHES ON BIKES
EDITED BY
ELLY BLUE